CLARA HUMBLE

and the
Not-So-Super
Powers

Anna Humphrey

Illustrations by Lisa Cinar

Owlkids Books

Owlkids Books acknowledges the financial support of the Canada Council for the Arts, the Ontario Arts Council, the Government of Canada through the Canada Book Fund (CBF), and the Government of Ontario through the Ontario Media Development Corporation's Book Initiative for our publishing activities.

Published in Canada by
Owlkids Books Inc.
10 Lower Spadina Avenue
Toronto, ON M5V 2Z2

Published in the United States by
Owlkids Books Inc.
1700 Fourth Street
Berkeley, CA 94710

Library and Archives Canada Cataloguing in Publication

Humphrey, Anna, 1979-, author
    Clara Humble and the not-so-super powers / written by Anna Humphrey ; illustrated by Lisa Cinar.

ISBN 978-1-77147-147-3 (hardback)

    I. Cinar, Lisa, 1980-, illustrator II. Title.

PS8615.U457C53 2016   jC813'.6   C2015-908054-1

Library of Congress Control Number: 2016930943

Edited by: Karen Li
Designed by: Barb Kelly

ONTARIO ARTS COUNCIL
CONSEIL DES ARTS DE L'ONTARIO
an Ontario government agency
un organisme du gouvernement de l'Ontario

Canada Council   Conseil des Arts
for the Arts   du Canada

Canadä

Manufactured in Altona, MB, Canada, in May 2016, by Friesens Corporation
Job #218807

A   B   C   D   E   F

 Publisher of Chirp, chickaDEE and OWL
www.owlkidsbooks.com

Owlkids Books is a division of  Bayard
CANADA

For YaYa & Gracie. Once neighbors, always family.
— A. H.

For Anabel and Margie, who also have secret super powers!
— L. C.

Contents

A Villain Gets Herself into Hot Water

I won't lie to you. Strange things had been going on for a while, but I didn't realize how truly exceptional I was until the day of the dancing-alligator attack. It was noon at the track and field semifinals. Top athletes from my school (Gledhill Elementary), our rival school (R.R. Reginald), and all the other elementary schools in the city of Gleason were gathered at Blinkstone Park.

We were supposed to be eating our packed lunches at the picnic tables near the duck pond, then doing our warm-up stretches while we waited for Coach Shipley to hand out the race numbers. But because I'm kind of a natural at the hundred-meter dash, I wasn't too worried about preparing.

Instead, I was putting the finishing touches on my newest comic strip: *@Cat & the Kibble Catastrophe*. In this action-packed episode,

@Cat (the hero, who's part-computer, part-cat, and all awesome) must once again use her cleverness, cuteness, and state-of-the-art circuitry to defeat her archenemy, Poodle Noodle (the villainous balloon-animal poodle):

@Cat was in a tight spot again, that was for sure, and I hated to leave her there…but my best friend, Bradley, was peering over my shoulder.

"Is she going to use her repulsor beam or her telescopic claws?" he asked.

I shrugged. I didn't really know yet. Even though I was her creator, @Cat often kept me guessing as much as she did her readers, which was fine with me. Not knowing the end of each adventure was my favorite part about writing it.

"Well…you should probably stop drawing and eat now anyway," Bradley pointed out reasonably. "I know you said you're a naturally fast runner, but it's important to load up on carbs before the race. For maximum energy."

He was right, of course. Bradley was always thinking ahead.

I unzipped my backpack, hoping my dad had remembered that I'd asked for pasta—but no such luck.

"What *is* that?" Bradley asked.

I pulled a bubblegum-pink bottle out of my lunch bag and

set it down on the picnic table. It was a recycled Pepto-Bismol container, but it was nestled in one of those foam drink holders that are supposed to keep cans of soda cold when you go on a picnic— except this bottle was steaming hot and there was a string coming out the top.

I held the thing, turning it quickly to keep my fingers from overheating. "I have no clue," I said. "It's practically boiling, though."

"Do you think it might explode?" Bradley's eyes went wide with hope.

A small explosion would have definitely been exciting, but even though my dad's packed lunches were sometimes unusual—leftover ground beef wrapped in lettuce leaves, macaroni and cheese stuffed into pita bread, half a toasted bagel with an egg cooked inside the hole—they'd never been dangerous before.

Normal Bradley face

Excited-about-minor-explosions face

"Doubt it," I said.

Still, I twisted the

top off carefully, just in case. The bottle was filled with hot water, and when I pulled on the string, I discovered that it was tied to something long and beige and wet: a hot dog.

"Look!" Bradley dug a wad of tinfoil out of my lunch bag. "I think your dad gave you a bun, too."

He was right.

"No ketchup, though," he reported gravely.

But it turned out lack of ketchup was the least of our problems just then. Because Bossy Becky McDougall—captain of the R.R. Reginald Raccoons and my only real rival in the hundred-meter dash—was coming right toward us. She pushed past our school mascot, the Gledhill Gator, without even saying "Excuse me" and came to a stop in front of us.

"Clara? *What* is *that*?" she asked, catching sight of my Pepto-Bismol bottle. "Are you sick?" She asked the last part with a half-smirky, half-hopeful look. Wouldn't it just make her day if a seriously upset stomach kept me from winning the blue ribbon in the hundred-meter dash?

"It's actually just a hot dog." I held up the wiener on its string.

"Not that." She stared at me like I was a doofus. "*That*," she said. "The pink bottle. We have it at home. It's for diarrhea." She paused dramatically, then looked around to make sure as many people as possible were listening. "Do you have diarrhea?"

"No!" I said quickly.

"That's even worse, then. You shouldn't take medicine if you're not sick."

It's always like that talking to Becky. You can't say *anything* without getting lectured. We were in the same Brownie pack for two years, so I'd know.

She'd boss the other Brownies whenever an adult wasn't looking, but the second the leaders turned around, she'd bat her long eyelashes, pretend like she was being SOOOOO nice, volunteer to make extra care packages for the children's hospital, and then get picked to lead the sharing circle.

"Well, whatever. Enjoy your lunch," Becky said, wrinkling her nose at my medicine/hot dog bottle. She did a shoulder stretch, then put one foot up on the picnic bench between me and Bradley, and brushed a microscopic speck of dirt off her prized silver running shoes. They were the same ones she'd made a huge deal about at the last track meet,

saying that they were the most aerodynamic shoes on the market, and that her dad got them for her in London, England, and that they were "real Italian leather, and a limited edition, and *very expensive,* so don't step on them, puh-*lease*."

Becky straightened up, then pointed at the Gledhill Gator, who had hopped up on a park bench. He was popping and locking in time to the music playing over the loudspeakers.

"Also," she added, "don't take this personally, but your crocodile has, like, zero rhythm."

Don't take it personally? When she'd just insulted the ultimate symbol of Gledhill Elementary's school spirit?!

"I won't take it personally," I answered, "because he's got ten times more rhythm than your rat." This was undeniably true.

There are some people who volunteer to be the team mascot because they think it's an easy way to get out of class for an afternoon. To them, it's about putting on an animal suit and sitting around drinking from the vat of super-sugary neon-orange energy drink that the grocery store donates to every track meet. The R.R. Reginald Raccoon is one of these people.

On the other hand, when Don Hu—the sixth-grader who's been our team mascot three years running—puts on his suit, he's so much more than a kid in an oversized animal costume.

The R.R. Reginald Raccoon

(Who looks more like a rat, if you ask me)

He *is* the Gator, body and soul. He busts out his best break-dance moves like his life depends on it, and whenever we score a victory, we know we owe our team spirit to the Gator and all that he stands for.

"Our mascot is a *raccoon*," Becky answered, shooting me an icy look. "And he can dance circles around your crocodile."

"*Alligator*," I corrected, but Becky didn't seem to hear me. She was already marching across the field toward her teammates.

"Honestly," I sighed, going back to my hot dog. "Some people!"

Bradley nodded and took a bite of his sandwich. I tried to finish my lunch quickly, hoping I'd have a few minutes to draw the next panel that would lead @Cat to certain victory and Poodle Noodle to definite defeat, but before I could get three bites in—

"Dance-off! Dance-off! Dance-off!"

Bradley was the first to hear the chant coming from the other side of the picnic area.

"Uh-oh," he said.

Several R.R. Reginald kids were walking toward us, pushing their ratty raccoon in front of them.

"Have no fear. I'll send that raccoon running." Don hopped off the bench. "Come on, Gledhill Gators," he called out in his booming voice.

What can I say? Where the Gator goes, we follow. The Gledhill kids started to cheer, and Bradley and I took our places near the front of the pack.

"Dance-off! Dance-off! Dance-off!"

The R.R. Reginald kids arrived at our tables near the pond, forming a semicircle. The Gledhill team made up the other half of the ring. A hush fell over the crowd.

"You ready, Raccoon?" the Gator challenged. His words were met with cheers from our team.

"Ummm…" The rat (I mean, raccoon) didn't sound ready at all, but Bossy Becky nudged him into the circle from behind, almost sending him sprawling onto the grass.

"Rodents first," said the Gator.

He stepped back gallantly, and the raccoon started dancing—if you could call it that. I'm more of a comic-book artist than a dance expert… but even I could tell that the routine wasn't great, since it mostly involved running around in a circle. It also didn't help that the mascot's head nearly flopped right off when he tried to finish his performance with a body wave.

"Not bad, not bad," Don said kindly. Then he took his time and did a few stretches before stepping into the circle. He waited until the beat was just right before beginning to nod his giant gator head in time to the music. Some of the

R.R. Reginald kids snickered, like they thought that was all he had, but our team knew better. The Gator was just getting in the zone. Suddenly he dropped to the ground and started spinning on his back in a full-out, jaw-dropping, foot-tapping break-dance routine.

"Yeah!" shouted Siu, our top long-distance runner.

"Show 'em who's got gattitude!" I added. (Get it? It's like attitude, but for gators.)

Never one to disappoint his adoring fans, the Gator jumped up in one smooth motion and shook his tail right in the R.R. Reginald kids' faces, then he added a few fancy foot spins.

"Go, Gator! Go, Gator! Go, Gator!" we chanted— which was probably what got Don pumped up enough to try his legendary one-armed handstand. It's a dangerous move at the best of times, but nearly impossible on uneven ground while wearing a forty-pound gator suit.

Still, he nailed it...or he would have if Becky hadn't taken matters into her own hands.

"Oops," she said loudly, throwing her ponytail elastic inside the circle. "Excuse me. Pardon me.

The incredibly awesome one-handed Gator-stand, one second before it all went wrong

Innocent ducks that have no idea what's about to hit them

I need to get that." She pushed through the crowd, and before I could guess what was going on in her supremely evil mind, she'd already yelled for backup.

"Come on, R.R. Reginald! Let's get him!"

All of a sudden, a pack of R.R. Reginald kids came charging at the Gator. Meanwhile, I just stood there with Bradley and the other Gledhill kids, frozen to the spot, watching in utter disbelief. For a second, Don wobbled slightly, and it looked like he might hand-stand his ground, but then his arm gave out and he fell on his side, rolled, and landed in the pond with an enormous splash. Slimy, muddy water and alarmed quacking ducks went flying in all directions.

Bradley, who has earned his lifesaver's badge in swimming, was the first one into the pond after Don. Two other boys from our team, plus Angela Langley, our star shot-putter, followed closely behind.

"Are you okay?" Bradley asked. All four kids were working together to pull off Don's gator head, which was quickly soaking up scummy pond water. It finally came loose, and Don emerged, looking shocked but unhurt. They all headed for shore, their feet making squelching sounds against the mucky bottom of the pond.

"Oh, thank goodness!" I heard an all-too-familiar voice say a second later. "He's okay!"

I turned, and there was Bossy Becky, leading her team's coach over.

Our coach, Coach Shipley, was running down the path right behind them.

"I went straight to get help from an adult when

I saw the crocodile fall in," Becky explained to nobody in particular, batting her eyelashes innocently. "I was *so worried!*"

"Don!" Coach Shipley said when she reached the edge of the pond. "What on earth happened here?"

"Come on, R.R. Reginald," Becky's coach said. "Looks like everything's under control. Let's get ready for our events and give the Gators some space."

Only it turned out that things weren't under control! Not at all! A few minutes later, the referee came over and told us that because four members of our team (not including the Gator) had wet, muddy clothes, they wouldn't be able to participate that day. That meant Bradley was out of the long jump, our two best hurdlers (Roger and Will) were disqualified, and Angela, our hands-down first-place contender at shot put, wouldn't be able to compete!

"It's so unfair!" Don said, wringing water out of his tail. "They pushed me in. You should disqualify those R.R. Reginald Rats instead." But none of the teachers were taking sides. Instead, they were reorganizing the event schedules as if the matter was already settled.

I was so mad I could have screamed—and
if Becky had been smart enough to leave me
alone, that's probably the worst that would have
happened…but, of course, she couldn't resist the
opportunity to rub it in.

"Sorry to hear so many of your teammates aren't
allowed to compete," she said, leaning over our
table a few minutes later.

She already had her race number pinned to her
shirt. Her friends Darla and Joanna were standing
behind her. They were sipping chocolate milk
through straws and smirking at us like smirking
was their full-time job.

"I guess our school will probably get the most
blue ribbons now. Next time, your crocodile
probably shouldn't dance so close to the pond,"
she added. "It's dangerous."

And that was her fateful mistake, because it
made me truly lose my patience.

"You *pushed* him," I said. "We all saw it. And for
the last time, he's an *alligator*!"

And *this* is where things started to get strange. I
felt my pulse quicken like my blood was boiling…
my fingertips and toes tingled with electricity…

the hairs on the back of my neck stood up…and without even really meaning to, I found myself facing injustice head on.

"You're making me angry!" I said. "And trust me, you don't want to do that."

Ears:
Supersonic
hearing
kicks in

Antenna:
Wi-Fi capabilities
engage

Heart:
Caring center
activated

Paws:
Telescopic
claws on
standby

When injustice rears its ugly head, @Cat can't help but heed the call—and neither can I.

Becky rolled her eyes to let me know that she wasn't scared in the least, but the joke was on her because the next thing I knew, my Pepto-Bismol bottle tipped, landing sideways on the picnic table, and a small waterfall of warm, stinky hot-dog water came splashing out, right onto her one-of-a-kind, genuine-Italian-leather, don't-step-on-them-puh-*lease* shoes.

"ACK!" Becky shouted. She backed up and threw her hands in the air, knocking a pinecone off the tree above her. It sailed in a perfect arc and landed *right* in Darla's chocolate milk with a plop and a splash that caught her square in the face. In her surprise, Darla dropped the carton and brown milk splashed all over her Reeboks.

"Oh my God!" Joanna said, rushing to Becky and Darla's rescue as if they'd been scalded with molten lava instead of splashed with a little hot-dog water and chocolate milk. "Are you guys *okay*?!"

"Ugggh," Becky said, shaking her foot and making a strangled sound. "My running shoes! They're soaked. And they smell disgusting!"

She was right. Hot-dog water *does* have a bad smell, which is weird, because hot dogs taste so good.

"Mine are drenched, too," Darla whined.

"Darn, your shoes are wet?" Don said with mock sadness. He was busy hanging his sopping gator costume over a tree branch. "You know the ref said nobody can compete in wet clothes, right? Gee. That sucks. I guess that means you're both out of the competition."

"You did this on purpose, Clara Humble!" Becky

said, pointing her finger at me. "I'm telling my coach!" And with that, she marched off to tell on me with Darla and Joanna following close behind.

Don walked over and put his arm around me. "As Gators, you know we usually play by the rules…but I have to say, she had that coming. Nice job, Clara!"

"And did you see how that pinecone flew?" said Eli, one of our long jumpers. He eyed the chocolate milk container, which Darla the litterbug had left behind on the ground. "Becky just throws her hands up. Then *whoosh*. BAM. A total slam dunk. What were the odds?"

It *had* been a total slam dunk. And despite the credit the Gator had given me, I was almost positive I hadn't touched the Pepto-Bismol bottle that had started the whole chain reaction. All the same, the entire series of events had been just a little too amazing to be a coincidence, if you asked me. I bent down, picked up my empty hot-dog bottle, screwed the top back on, and put it in my lunch bag.

Like I said, it wasn't my first clue that there might be more to me than met the eye…but it was definitely my biggest one yet.

A Night Too Sad to Be Saved?

We worked hard that afternoon. By the end of the track meet, we had six blue ribbons—including the one I wore pinned to my shirt. Not bad for a team that had lost almost half its best athletes *and* its Gator mascot to sabotage. Meanwhile, R.R. Reginald took home eight first places, but you'd think it was fifty, the way Becky and her friends bragged.

"I'll see you at the finals, Clara," she had called out to me when we were handing back our race numbers. She was carrying her prized silver running shoes in a plastic bag. "And when I do, the next blue ribbon's mine!"

I didn't even bother to make a comeback (I was pretty worn out, you know, from all the *winning* I'd just done), plus my mind was buzzing, thinking about the strange hot-dog water incident and what it might mean.

As soon as we got back to school, it was time to get our things and board our regular buses. Bradley's little sister, Val, had fallen at second recess and wanted to tell him everything and show him her Band-Aid. So while he sat down beside her to hear all about it, I snuck away to the back of the bus, threw my bag down on a seat, and took out my sketchbook. I opened it to a fresh page and started writing a list—a list of clues and evidence, to be exact.

Val's Scraped Knee Saga must have been really impressive, because we were almost at our stop when Bradley finally came down the aisle and slid into the seat beside me.

"Whatcha doing?" he asked.

I closed my sketchbook. "Starting math homework."

It wasn't that I didn't want to tell Bradley about the theory that was forming in my mind, or the clues I'd been writing down that helped prove it. I *knew* he'd be excited for me. I just didn't want to tell him on the bus. You could never be sure when villains might be lurking and listening in. Also, I wanted to be certain first. Which meant gathering more evidence.

"Want help with the division?" Bradley asked.

I shook my head. Even if I *had* been doing my long division, I wouldn't have asked him for help. Bradley is quiet and careful. His factors and dividends drop down in straight lines with the remainders tucked at the top like birds on a wire. My numbers spill sideways across the page, like they're trying to run away. Plus I usually get the wrong answer—but it's *not* my fault. Math was made for people who think in straight lines and take things one step at a time, like Bradley.

I, on the other hand, am a "creative," "impulsive," "big picture" person—or at least that's how my teachers explain why I'm sometimes drawing instead of paying attention in class.

According to my mom, it also means I take after my dad. He gets an idea in his head, and then he forgets about everything else while he tries to make it happen, even if he doesn't always have an exact plan for how it's going to work.

"Our stop!" Bradley announced.

Bradley and Val's babysitter (whose name is Svetlana) was waiting on the corner. She was texting, but she tucked her phone into her pocket when she saw us.

"Hi, kids. How was track and field?" Without waiting for an answer, she smushed Val and then Bradley into oblivion in her super-strong Pilates-toned arms. Bradley really needed to put his foot down and outlaw bus-stop hugs. Half the school was watching through the bus window.

"Good." Bradley shrugged, wriggling away.

"Hello, Clara," Svetlana said. I smiled. Bus-stop hugs aside, I liked her. She always wore thick blue eyeliner that curled up at the edges. It made her look like an Egyptian pharaoh.

Sometimes I couldn't help feeling kind of jealous that Bradley had someone waiting for him. Since I'd turned nine that summer, my dad had decided I was old enough to walk home from the bus stop alone.

It wasn't far, but there was this one old, twisted tree I had to pass. Huge scary birds with black feathers liked to nest in its terrible branches. And every single time, just when you were walking along thinking what a lovely peaceful day it was, they'd flap their giant wings at you, squawk *BA-CAAAAW*, and make you almost pee your pants.

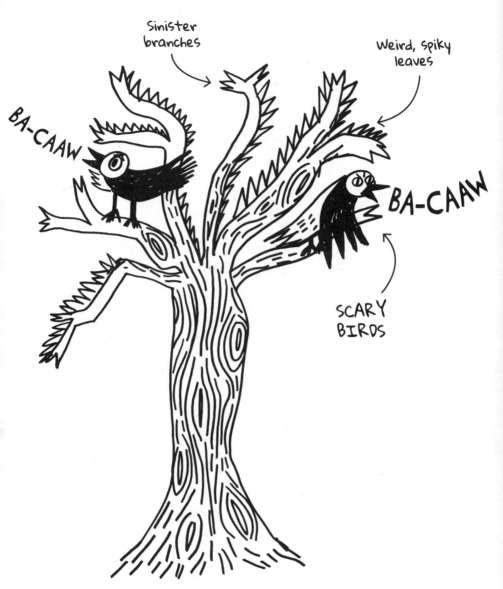

Sinister branches

Weird, spiky leaves

BA-CAAW

BA-CAAW

SCARY BIRDS

"See you after dinner?" Bradley asked.

It was one of those questions that isn't a question.

I *always* went over after dinner. I nodded anyway,

then I ran, holding my breath until I got safely past the bird tree and my house came into sight.

My neighbor Momo was out in her yard, bent over near her rose bushes. Because she was wearing bright yellow pants, her bum looked like a big sun rising up in the air.

"Hello, dingbat!" I called as I got nearer.

She straightened and smiled. "Hey there, koo-koo-bird." Momo brushed one of her gardening gloves against her thigh, leaving a bunch of brambly things behind. "How was the big meet?"

I lifted up the blue ribbon attached to my shirt to show her, and she held out her hand for a high-five.

"That's my girl!" she said, beaming.

Momo had been living next door to us since before I could remember. My parents say I was two years old when I started letting myself in through her back door, which she always leaves unlocked. I couldn't say her name (Maureen) back then, and that's why she's Momo to this day. She might be old, but—don't tell Bradley this—she's my other best friend.

My parents are always busy being parents, but Momo has time to watch caterpillars, or walk to the corner store for popsicles, or build snow forts, or sit around playing Go Fish and Spit. She's like a grandma, only she never talks about arthritis, hardly ever asks about my grades, and always looks through the bag with me to choose the cookies with the most icing. Basically, she's the youngest old person I know.

"We won six blue ribbons in all," I said.

Of course I wanted to tell Momo about Bossy Becky and the hot-dog water, too, but as fun as she is, Momo is still an adult, which means she sometimes has to be *responsible*. If she heard about Becky pushing the Gator, she'd probably get worried about bullying. She'd also say something *sensible*, like that Becky acts that way because she's insecure, which isn't true. Some people are just mean.

And as for the theory I was working on, well, I couldn't risk telling anyone until I was certain. Momo believes in guardian angels and thinks ladybugs are good luck, but even she might think I was going nuts.

Instead, I changed the subject. "Why are you doing that?" I asked.

Momo's garden was the best on our street. It was full of dinner-plate-sized sunflowers and magnificent morning glories. But it was early October, and the leaves and vines were starting to shrivel. She'd pulled them off her fence and shoved them into tall paper yard-waste bags. Momo didn't usually do that before winter. She said the dried vines gave the little birds shelter from the wind and snow.

"Just a little fall cleanup," she said, and I didn't even have time to ask her what the little birds would do before—

"Gotcha!" she yelled, tossing two big handfuls of garden scraps at me.

"Momo!" I batted the brambles and leaves away. Then I pretended to bend to clean up the spilled stuff, but the second she crouched down to help, I made a lunge for a handful of dried vines from an open bag and dumped them all over her head.

She looked up through the twiggy mess that hung down from her snow-white hair. "You… little…brat." Her mouth was hanging open, but her eyes were smiling.

I ran backward. "Who are you calling a brat,

brat?" It was one of the things we always said. We had about a million of them. Like how, instead of saying "excuse me," we always said "scoozi," and how we made up funny names for Momo's cats. Fatty-Fatty-Two-Tip is a huge orange tomcat with little white patches on his ears that make it look like he's been turned upside down and dipped in paint. Wiggles is a gray one who's always rolling in the grass.

Momo grabbed another armful of yard waste and threw it at me.

What choice did I have but to fight back?

Between the two of us, we emptied nearly an entire bag and were covered in dirt and weeds before Momo started gasping for breath. "Okay." She held out her hands. "Mercy! Help me clean this up, kid." So I did, then Momo glanced at her watch and said I'd better go inside before my dad got worried.

I picked up my backpack. "Keep it loose, Mother Goose!" It was another thing we always said.

Momo paused and cleared her throat. Then she rubbed at her eye, like maybe she had a bit of leaf caught in it. "Take care, Polar Bear," she answered.

"I'm home and I'm hungry!" I called when I got inside.

"In here!" my dad answered. The door we use to get to the garage through the laundry room was open, so I followed the sound of his voice.

I found my dad standing on the top rung of a ladder, using a screwdriver while holding some wires in his teeth. He was wearing a button-up shirt and dress pants, which meant he'd had a job interview that day. But his clothes were covered in cobwebs and dust, which meant he'd been in the garage and hard at work for a while, making whatever it was he was making.

"I'm fixing this garage door opener once and for all," he explained when he'd finished attaching a small black box to the ceiling. "Yesterday I noticed that we still had parts from that old home security system sitting around in the basement, and today when I pulled into the driveway and the button didn't work—"

"Like always," I supplied.

"Like always," he agreed. "Anyway, I decided it was high time to do something about it and put those parts to good use while I was at it. Check this out and imagine the ease." He climbed off the ladder and heaved the heavy garage door open, grunting with the effort. It was the way we opened and closed it, since the remote we kept in the car never worked.

He motioned for me to step outside, then yanked the door down behind us. "Your mother will pull into the driveway," he said, pointing up. "This sensor will communicate wirelessly with a device I'll attach to the windshield." He reached into his pocket and pulled out a circuit board. "And presto!"

The door gave a groan and lurched upward.

"She's in!"

The hinges creaked and the wood shuddered as the door snagged and came to a stop about a foot off the ground.

"Well, it needs a little grease." My dad laughed. "But you get the idea." He ruffled my hair. "Snack's waiting for you in the fridge," he said. "I'll be right in."

"Okay, see you soon," I said, even though I knew it wasn't true. When my dad got started on one of his inventions, he tended to lose track of time. I wouldn't see him until dinner. Not that I minded, really. I had important secret stuff to do.

After I ate my snack (pineapple chunks and corn chips), I filled three plastic cups with water and then carried them carefully up the stairs to the spare room. It's my favorite place for thinking and drawing. It's quieter than my room, where Bijou (my pet chinchilla) is always chattering away in her cage or wanting to be held. Plus I keep my comic books there. Bijou is a bit of a paper chewer, and I'm not willing to risk her getting at my collection—especially the rare ones, like *The Amazing Spider-Man #300*.

I lined the plastic cups up on the windowsill, grabbed a bunch of towels from the hall closet to put on the floor underneath, then sat down on the bed and started to focus all my energy on them. First I tried staring at the glasses. And when that

Me looking @Cat-menacing!

didn't work, I raised my hands over my head and looked menacing, like @Cat does right before she bares her ferocious telescopic claws.

But looking menacing is hard work (for one thing, it uses a lot of eyebrow muscles), and after a few minutes, I got tired. I gave up and went to get my sketchbook.

When we last saw @Cat she was trapped on the other side of the lake, helpless to stop Poodle Noodle as he floated across to blow up the cat food factory—but was she *really* helpless? One thing about heroes: no matter what obstacles they face, they find a way to prevail.

I had just finished perfecting the look of disappointment on Poodle Noodle's face when I heard my mom's voice, clear as a bell, from all the way downstairs. I happen to have excellent hearing. At least 20/20. (I once heard my dad opening a bag of cookies in the kitchen from all the way across the backyard with the door closed.) And okay, I guess it didn't hurt that the heating duct in the spare room goes pretty much straight down to the kitchen.

"How did your interview go?" my mom asked.

My dad didn't answer for a while. I could hear the sound of pots banging around, which meant he'd been so busy working on his garage door opener that he'd forgotten to start dinner. Nothing unusual there.

"Not bad," Dad answered. "They said they've got a few other candidates to interview, though. And you know, the more I think about it"—the fridge door opened, then closed again—"the more I wonder if it isn't too far from home. With the commute," my dad went on, "I'd be cutting it pretty close to get home in time for Clara. I mean, we could ask Momo to watch her after school, but I just wonder…"

My mom sighed. At first, I figured it was because my dad didn't want the job—he'd been looking for work for almost a month and had turned down two jobs already because they didn't "seem up his alley"—but this turned out to be something *much* worse.

"Actually, for once, we can't ask Momo to watch Clara," my mom said. "I was talking to her on my way in. She's putting her house on the market."

"What?!" my dad said.

I leaned in closer to the vent. Putting her house on the market? What did that mean?

"She went on a tour of a retirement community in Bowmanville. It's a place where she can have a small garden and keep the cats. She says she wants to break the news to Clara herself."

"Oh no!" my dad exclaimed.

"Oh no!" I cried, then I clapped a hand over my mouth—even though being overheard by my parents was the least of my worries. Momo was leaving me? For a retirement community? What was she going to *do* there with all the old people? They weren't going to build snow forts or eat giant cherry lollipops with her. She wouldn't fit in! And worse still, what was *I* going to do without her?

"Clara's going to be devastated," my dad said.

"I know," Mom agreed. "God, *I'm* devastated. It's going to feel strange not having Momo next door."

More pots banged. The fridge opened and closed a few more times, then they started talking about whether to put bean sprouts in the salad—as if bean sprouts even mattered when the entire world was about to fall apart.

At dinner, it was more of the same.

We were having Dad's late-week specialty—*chicken à la things* (chicken plus whatever things are lingering in the fridge by Thursday night). That night, it was barbecue sauce, carrots, and frozen peas. As we ate it, my parents talked about my uncle's condo fees, argued about the rules of table tennis, and asked each other to pass the salad. Nobody even said Momo's name or noticed that I was hardly touching my food.

"I can't believe I haven't asked yet!" Dad said all of a sudden. "How was the track meet?"

"Good," I mumbled miserably, stabbing a cooked carrot. "I won the blue ribbon for the hundred-meter dash."

They exchanged a worried look. My parents aren't exactly sporty people.

"Blue is very good, Clara," my mom said finally. "You should be proud! If you keep practicing, maybe you'll win the red one next time."

"Blue is first place," I told her.

"Oh…well, then. Even better!" she said. "We should celebrate. How about I bake you some spelt chocolate chip muffins after dinner?"

I didn't want to hurt my mom's feelings, so I stopped myself from pointing out that spelt muffins aren't a good way to celebrate *anything*.

Not that it mattered. I didn't feel much like celebrating, anyway. Even though Becky had deserved hot-dog-water shoes for what she did to the Gator, and even though I'd been happy with my blue ribbon at first, the victory felt kind of hollow now. For one thing, because Becky hadn't competed, I didn't get the chance to beat her fair and square. Also, since I'd heard the news about Momo, I was pretty sure I'd never smile about anything ever again.

One of these things is not like the others:

SPELT MUFFIN

ROCK IN A MUFFIN CUP

ACTUALLY DELICIOUS MUFFIN

"Mmmmmm. Spelt," my dad said, grinning at me.

Mom smacked him in the arm. "Clara loves my spelt muffins," she said.

I went back to stabbing my carrots. I knew it wasn't my parents' fault. They didn't want Momo to move any more than I did. And they would have told me the news if she hadn't wanted to do it herself...but for some reason, none of that seemed to matter. I couldn't help feeling mad at them for keeping such a terrible secret from me and for carrying on like everything was fine.

I scrunched my hands into little balls and glared at my plate. Tears of rage clouded my eyes and then, just like that afternoon, without any warning—

"Oh, Clara!" My mom stood up, backing away from the milk that was spreading across the table, away from my tipped-over glass. "Not again!"

My mouth dropped open. I was 99 percent sure that I hadn't touched the Pepto-Bismol bottle at the track meet. But this time, I was absolutely certain I hadn't touched my milk glass.

"Sorry," I said, standing up to get the dish towel.

"Oh, that's okay." My mom sighed and waved me back toward my seat. "I'll get it. Just try to be more careful, okay?"

"Okay," I grumbled, cutting into my chicken. But the truth was, I wasn't feeling quite so grumbly inside anymore. I was still mad and still frustrated, but underneath all that, excitement was bubbling up. I'd been looking for more proof, hadn't I? And now I had it.

A Hero Is Born

After Mom finished cleaning up my spilled milk, my parents went right back to talking about things like tax receipts and vacuum bags, but I was too excited by what I'd just discovered to care. I wolfed down the rest of my *chicken à la things* and asked to be excused.

"I'll be at Bradley's, okay?" I said loudly. I was already in the front hall, pulling on my boots.

"Put on a hat," my mom said. "The evenings are getting chilly."

"And be home by—"

I'm pretty sure my dad would have said "dark," but he was interrupted by a loud groaning noise. The walls shook and the keys on the hallway key-hook thing rattled.

"What the—?" Dad said, getting up and going to the front window. "The garage door just opened by

Shakin' it!

Dad's hula-girl keychain

TO DO:
- BUY MILK
- FIX GARAGE DOOR

itself. Something must have triggered the sensor."
He opened the front door and leaned out. "It didn't
get stuck, though. It went all the way up."

"Well, that's progress." My mom started to clear
the dishes.

"You've got your boots on, Clara," my dad said.
"Would you pull the door closed on your way out?"

Under normal circumstances, I would have
complained (our garage door weighs ten tons and
goes down as easily as an elephant on a waterslide),
but I was dying to get to Bradley's and tell him my
news, so instead, I just did it—then I ran around
the house and across our backyard and wiggled
through the gap between our fence and Bradley's.

"Hello?" I called out.

"Over here," he answered. Bradley was sitting deep inside our third giant hole. The pom-pom of his hat was poking out the top. "I think I found something new. It's silver," he said.

I stepped into the hole beside him and crouched down.

"We should scrape around the outside first so we don't damage it. Remember what the archeology book said?" Bradley added.

I found my shovel in our toolbox and started to gently chip away at the earth on one side while Bradley did the other. At first I thought the object was probably just an old bottle cap, but the more we dug, the more it looked like something actually interesting. A tin bowl, maybe, or some kind of box? When Bradley turned away to mark the spot on the grid he was drawing, I tried to pry it out with the tip of my shovel. I knew Bradley's archeology book wouldn't approve, but the "correct" way of digging was *so* slow.

"Guess what?" I said, after we'd been scraping at the dirt for approximately forever. I thought I might explode from excitement if I didn't tell him right that second.

"You're getting a kitten!" he said.

I put "kitten" at the top of my Christmas and birthday lists every year, but my parents always said that a chinchilla was more than enough pet for now.

"I wish," I said. "Good guess. Try again…It's something *super*." I raised my eyebrows, hoping he'd catch my meaning.

"Oh! You finished @*Cat & the Kibble Catastrophe*," he said. "Did you bring it for me to read?"

"Well…yes, I finished. But I didn't bring it. And that's not it. Guess again. Remember— something *super*."

"Your mom's taking you to SuperShop for new running shoes for the final track meet?" he tried. "You fixed that broken part of your bed with superglue?" I shook my head. "You're super excited about the blue ribbon you won?"

I sighed. "Never mind! I'll just tell you. Come closer."

He leaned in.

"I think I have super powers," I whispered. There was something thrilling about saying it out loud at last.

I couldn't tell if the look on Bradley's face was more shocked than amazed or more amazed than shocked, so I went on. "I've been suspecting it for a while, but today, when my hot-dog water tipped right on Becky's shoe and then the pinecone landed in Darla's chocolate milk…I mean, what were the odds? A million to one?"

"Probably…" Bradley said, squinting at me.

"A million to one," I repeated. "Wouldn't you say that's too small for it to be a coincidence?"

Bradley nodded, like he was giving it some serious thought. "Hmmm," he said.

"I mean, I wasn't a hundred percent sure at first. But then tonight, at dinner, I was so mad at my mom and dad, and out of nowhere, I spilled my milk. And *I wasn't even touching it!*"

"But you always spill your milk at dinner," Bradley said.

"Exactly!" I agreed. "That's what I mean. It's been going on for ages! I just never put the pieces together."

"So your super power is spilling milk?"

"Not just milk, Bradley. I can spill anything!"

Bradley started to dig faster. He was probably

hoping to hide it, but I could see the corners of his mouth turning up in a small smile.

"You don't believe me," I said flatly.

"Sure I do," he answered too quickly.

"You're trying not to laugh," I pointed out.

"It just…sounded funny at first," he explained. "I mean, a little. Aren't super powers usually things like flying? Or shooting strings out your wrists?"

"Those are *spiderwebs*," I said, getting a little annoyed now. "That's why they call him Spider-Man. And that's a cartoon. Just like @Cat. I'm not crazy. I'm not saying I have jet-pack paws. Or built-in Wi-Fi capabilities. Or that I can barf data clouds."

Is @Cat coughing up hairballs?
NO! WAIT! Those are
billion-megabyte data clouds!

"Anyway," I went on, "not all super powers are that amazing when you really stop and look at them. The Incredible Hulk lifts heavy stuff. Iceman makes things cold. Batman doesn't even *have* powers, unless you count dressing like a bat and owning a fast car, and *he* gets the job done." I was almost breathless as I delivered this speech, but the more I talked, the truer the words sounded. I just needed to make Bradley see! "Everyone knows it's not the size of the super power that counts—it's how you *use* it to defeat your opponent. It's about *brains* and *bravery* more than anything."

I could tell that Bradley was considering things carefully—like he always does. He definitely wasn't laughing anymore. He was starting to believe me. I mean, how could he not? There's no denying that superheroes bring bad guys to justice using whatever powers they've got. When they see evil, they can't help but take action…which, the more I thought about it, was a lot like me with Becky, wasn't it?

"And anyway, it's not just spilling stuff," I told Bradley. "I made a list."

I knew that if nothing else I'd said had worked,

this would prove it. Bradley loved lists more than anyone. I took a crumpled piece of paper from my pocket and handed it to him. It was the evidence I'd jotted down on the bus earlier that day.

"Look!" I said.

Clara Humble's Super Powers:
1 - The power to make stuff spill.
   (And all these years, my parents thought
   I was just clumsy!)
2 - Supersonic hearing.
3 - The power to communicate with chinchillas.
4 - The power to wake up at exactly 7:14
   every morning. No earlier, no later. Even
   on weekends. Even without an alarm clock.

"And that's just the beginning," I said when he'd finished reading. "There could be more!"

"Huh," Bradley said. "I knew you could do a lot of those things. I just never thought about them as super powers before." He set his shovel down. "And at first, I guess I wondered if there could be a lot of explanations for spilling things. Like, maybe somebody's arm knocked it."

I sighed. "I told you. I didn't even touch the bottle with the hot-dog water in it *or* my milk!"

I didn't say it out loud, but I couldn't help thinking that there could also be a lot of explanations for how a rusty short-handled spatula and a beer bottle with a pirate label had ended up buried in Bradley's backyard. Ever since we'd found these "treasures," Bradley had been convinced there must be even more pirate treasure nearby—and it wasn't that I thought it was impossible... but I'd had my doubts, too.

YARRRR! Flip me flapjacks and shiver me timbers!

According to Bradley, "Even olden-days pirates would have needed spatulas."

"You've heard that the human brain is more powerful than any computer, right?" I continued. "Some people might be able to use parts of their brains others can't... in ways science hasn't even imagined yet."

"Yeah. You're probably right." He shrugged, then dug a little more. "Have you told anyone else yet?"

"Why would I do that?"

"Well, if you have super powers…that's a big responsibility."

It was nice of Bradley to worry about me, but as one of @Cat's biggest fans, he should have known more about how super powers work. You can't just come out and *tell* people you have them. That's why all superheroes have alter egos. Spider-Man is Peter Parker. Superman is Clark Kent. @Cat ties a bow over her Wi-Fi antennae and masquerades as Fuzzy-Wuzzy-Snowball, an innocent house cat, to hide her true identity from the human world.

"I don't think anyone else would really understand. Especially not my parents," I pointed out.

"What about Momo, then?" Bradley suggested.

I took a deep breath and sighed it out. It wasn't that I'd forgotten the horrible news. I'd just been distracted by the super power stuff. And also trying my hardest to believe Momo wasn't really about to leave me.

"I don't think she'd understand, either," I said. "Plus she's going to be kind of busy with other stuff…" I told him the news about Momo moving.

"What?!" Bradley put his shovel down and sat back on his heels. "But she'll be so BORED at a nursing home! Trust me. My grandma's in one. All they do is play Bingo and watch a big fish tank. They're not even tropical fish. Just orange ones."

Bradley wasn't as close to Momo as I was, but they were friends, too. I knew he'd be upset by the news, but I hadn't guessed he'd be almost as devastated as I was.

"What are we going to *do*?" he asked, scratching underneath his hat. At first, I thought he was saying it like an expression—but then I noticed he was watching me intently, like he expected me to have an actual answer.

Obviously, I didn't. There was nothing we *could* do. Momo was an adult—which meant she got to do whatever she wanted, even if that included selling her house and leaving me behind. We were kids—which meant we just had to deal with whatever the adults decided to do, even though it was totally unfair.

Or *did* we just have to deal with it?! The realization hit me like a bolt of lightning.

THE FATEFUL DAY FUZZY-WUZZY WAS **TRANSFORMED** INTO @CAT

SHOO, CAT! I'm trying to write my prize-winning novel.

Meanwhile outside, a strange solar storm was brewing!

SIGH!

59

Wasn't fighting injustice what super powers were for? And wasn't the idea of Momo watching a fish tank all day while I wallowed around in utter loneliness just about as unjust as it got?

"What do you think @Cat would do?" I wondered out loud.

"I don't know..." Bradley answered.

Using all the strength in my fingers, I reached in and tugged at the edge of the silver thing in our hole. It came out with some clumps of earth, a few roots, and a large worm hanging off it. I brushed away the worm and muck to reveal a round tin, slightly rusted.

Now, I'm the last person to be superstitious, but there was no denying this was a sign.

"I don't know, either," I answered. "But I can tell you this much: she wouldn't take it lying down."

An Imminent
Invasion of Rats

Being a real-life superhero is *not* easy. I learned
that right off the bat, when I got home from
Bradley's that night. For one thing, there are *so
many* competing demands.

"Clara." My mom came up the basement stairs,
carrying a bag of wood chips. "You need to clean
Bijou's cage tonight. It's starting to smell again."

"Can I do it this weekend?" I whined. I needed
time to think of a really awesome superhero name
for myself. I also had to come up with a plan to
stop Momo from moving. Not to mention that
I had two pages of long division homework, and I
still didn't really understand how to do remainders.

"It's been almost a week," my mom said, handing
me the wood chips. "You're supposed to do it
every three days. *Without being reminded.* That
was the deal."

Of course I remembered the chinchilla deal. (How could I forget? My parents had even typed it up in a fancy font and made me sign a copy before we'd gone to the pet store.) Still, it seemed unfair. @Cat never has to clean up poop (that's what she keeps the humans around for). And can you picture Batman doing anything as ordinary as taking out the trash? Or folding laundry? Would Wonder Woman do long division while the world waited to be saved?

But I took the wood chips without any more protest. I'm a caring (if busy) pet owner. And as you might remember from the list of powers I made, I'm a little bit telepathic when it comes to chinchillas, or at least when it comes to *my* chinchilla. I knew for a fact that it made Bijou

CHINCHILLA MOOD DIAGRAM

HAPPY because:
- food
- clean cage
- snuggles

CRANKY because:
- no food
- smelly cage
- not feelin' the love

JUST CHILLIN' because:
- ate soooo much
- that's what Bijou does best
- about to fall asleep

cranky when her cage got smelly. I can always sense how she's feeling, and I'm really good at training her to do tricks—even though chinchillas *aren't* easy to train.

As soon as I went into my room, Bijou climbed onto her jungle gym and started hopping around in her cage. "Hi, goofball," I said. She held up her little paws like she was blowing a kiss. I picked her up gently and let her sniff my nose before setting her down on the floor.

"Here," I said. I climbed onto my desk and set a few raisins along the top of my curtain rod for incentive. "Practice your climbing. I've got work to do."

While Bijou climbed, I pulled the base of the cage out, dumped the mess in the garbage, and started wiping it down with a spray bottle filled with vinegar and water. And as I worked, I plotted.

WAYS TO USE MY SUPER POWERS TO KEEP MOMO FROM MOVING

1. Using my power to spill things...
I can make Momo spill her tea all over some kind of official house-selling document (except she could probably just print off another copy).

2. Using my supersonic hearing...
I can be the first to overhear Momo's moving date, plus all the other details, so that I can put a stop to it... somehow.

3. Using my power to communicate with chinchillas...I can...well, maybe I need to give that one some more thought, too.

4. Using my power to wake up at 7:14! Exactly! I can, ummm...I don't know... Come to think of it, that power hasn't come in handy for anything yet.

I dumped half the bag of pine shavings into the clean cage and breathed in their Christmassy smell. It was usually the best part of the job, but now thinking of the holidays only made me sad. I stared at the list of ideas I'd jotted down. Unless I could come up with a *much* better plan, Momo would be long gone before Christmas. With such small powers, there wouldn't be anything I could do to stop her!

I got back up on my desk and pulled Bijou off the curtains. "Oh, Bijou." I buried my face in her supersoft, velvety fur, which is perfect for soaking up tears. "What are we going to do?"

She chattered then gnawed softly on the collar of my shirt, which was her way of telling me she didn't know either, but that she hated to see me so sad.

I tossed and turned and worried most of the night, but still I woke up at 7:14! Exactly! That meant I was ready for school early, as usual.

Since I was in no rush to get to the bus, I crossed the street so I wouldn't have to walk under the terrible tree. Still, even though I was nowhere near it, a big red-eyed bird hopped out to the very edge of a branch and flapped its dark wings at me threateningly. I hooked my fingers under my backpack straps and ran the rest of the way.

Once I was at the bus stop, I stared hard at the porch light of the house across the street—just to test out another theory that had been forming in my mind.

"Clara? Are you okay?" I wasn't sure how much time had passed, but I'd been concentrating so hard that I hadn't noticed Bradley, his little sister, Val, and Svetlana arriving at the bus stop.

"Shhhh," I whispered to Bradley, not breaking my gaze. "Did you just see that light flicker?"

"Mrs. Campbell's light? On the blue house? Maybe," he said. "Wait. Definitely. And now it went off."

"Ha!" I said, grinning.

By now, the bus was coming down the street. Svetlana fussed with Val's ladybug hat, then smushed her into a hug.

"Have a good day, cutie," she said. When she was done, she came after Bradley, who was looking down at his feet, trying to avoid making eye contact with the kids on the bus. "Bradley, baby! What?! You don't give Svetlana a kiss anymore?" Svetlana pointed to her cheek. Bradley closed his eyes and gave her the fastest-ever peck. Then he stumbled up the bus stairs, his face bright red. I followed behind, glaring hard at two third-graders in the front seat, daring them to laugh.

"So what do you think?" I said as soon as we sat down. "About Mrs. Campbell's light?" I prompted when he gave me a blank stare.

"What about it?"

"How I burned it out," I whispered. "I never realized it before…but my mom is always saying that she can't buy lightbulbs for my room fast enough. Batteries, too! We have to buy them in twenty packs. I think it might be another power."

"Electromagnetism," Bradley said, his eyes going wide.

Sometimes Bradley cracks me up. I mean, how can he know a word like that, but not know that Spider-Man shoots spiderwebs out his wrists? As if to answer my question, he unzipped his backpack, pulled out a big yellow envelope, and handed it to me. It weighed as much as a dictionary.

"It's a little research I did on the Internet last night," he explained. He whispered the next part. "About real-life super powers. Telekinesis, psychokinesis, chlorokinesis, clairvoyance, electromagnetism…and those are just a few." He gave me a serious look. "Clara, you're not alone. There are people all over the world who are just like you. There could even be others…right on this bus!"

I glanced around. There was Jehan, making farting noises with his armpits. Clarence was blowing baseball-sized bubbles with a piece of gum. Sakura was biting her fingernails down to little stubs. They all seemed pretty normal to me.

"But that's not even the best news," Bradley went on. "If you have powers naturally, you can learn to control them *and* make them stronger. It's all about believing in yourself." He shrugged, then glanced down at his knees. "Plus it doesn't hurt to have a personal superhero trainer."

"You mean you?"

"Well, yeah," he said. "Who else? I *have* done a bit of research on the topic." He glanced at the enormous envelope. "What do you say, Super Clara?"

Super Clara? The name was simple, yet strong. I liked it. Actually, I liked it *a lot*. And Bradley was right. I needed to build my powers if they were going to do me (or Momo) any good, and I wasn't sure I could do it alone.

"Okay," I said. "What's our first step?"

As it turned out, Bradley already had a rigorous superhero training schedule planned for me. He'd even typed it up on the computer using a font called Comic Sans with extra information in "*super*script." That's classic Bradley, by the way. He's all about the details.

I couldn't wait to read it over, but I didn't end up having a chance until morning recess—because first thing after announcements, Principal Franco dropped some news on us that was so terrible it made thinking about anything else impossible.

"Don't take out your math books just yet," our teacher, Mrs. Smith, told us. "We're heading to the gym for a special assembly."

This one time last year, a kid in grade two drew a poster about healthy eating and submitted it to a contest at the grocery store. As first prize, she won a special dance presentation for her school where these overly happy adults wearing matching T-shirts sang us songs about green vegetables.

"Maybe it's an assembly about orange vegetables this time," Bradley said as we lined up at the door.

"Or maybe they're using the Fun-fest Fundraiser money to buy new playground equipment," Eric Richardson suggested hopefully, "and they want to tell us all about it."

It was true that our monkey bars were so rusty they left brown marks all over your hands, and that our climber was beyond babyish. I kind of hoped Eric was right…but it turned out he wasn't. At all.

"Boys and girls," Principal Franco said, holding up her hand for silence once we were all sitting on the gym floor. "Boys and girls," she said again, louder, when nobody listened. Finally, she had to shout it at the top of her lungs to get our attention.

"I'm sure you're wondering why I called you all here today," she said after the noise had quieted to a dull roar. "I have some important news to share, and I need everybody's undivided attention. Yesterday afternoon, I got a call from Principal Demerit, from our neighboring school, R.R. Reginald…"

"No way," Don Hu, who was sitting behind us, whispered.

I knew exactly what he was thinking. The assembly was going to be about what had happened to him at the track meet. News about the Gator's "swim" in the pond had spread through the Gledhill hallways quickly, and everyone was outraged.

Principal Demerit probably called to apologize for the R.R. Reginald Raccoons' unacceptable behavior and to tell us how they'd be severely punished. (My cousin had Ms. Demerit for a teacher once, before she was a principal. He said she was so strict that half the class had detention every day.) Maybe justice—I mean, besides the hot-dog-water vigilante type—was actually going to be done for once!

"Shhhh," Principal Franco said, holding up her hand again to silence the murmurs that were rippling around the gym. "Yesterday, mold was discovered in the walls at R.R. Reginald."

"Ha!" Don Hu said. "Serves them right."

Okay...so I had to admit, I was disappointed that Bossy Becky and her classmates weren't being forced to apologize for pushing the Gator into the slimy duck pond, but this was the next best thing. I turned to smile at Don. "The walls are probably full of moldy cheese. Perfect for a school full of rats, right?"

He laughed, then whispered what I'd just said to Sakura, who smiled and passed it on. Not to brag, but I *am* pretty hilarious sometimes.

"Mold is a serious health concern," Principal Franco went on. "Until it can be fixed, the building isn't safe. In the meantime, the students of R.R. Reginald are going to need a place to learn, which is why, starting on Monday, we'll be opening our doors to them until their own school can be repaired."

At that, a grumbling broke out in the gym that

no amount of teachers holding up their hands could ever hope to silence:

"What?"

"She can't be serious!?"

"They're coming *here*?"

"After what they did to our Gator?"

"There's *no* way."

Finally Mrs. Shipley, our coach and PE teacher, had to flick off the lights, sending the gym into total darkness. It made a whole bunch of kindergarteners and first-graders scream, but when she flicked them back on, Principal Franco was able to go on.

"I understand that some of you aren't pleased about this arrangement," she said, "especially in light of the incident at yesterday's track meet. But our neighbor is in need, and we must let bygones be bygones. I'm counting on all of you to give the R.R. Reginald students a big Gledhill welcome and make them feel at home over the coming months."

"Months?!" somebody shouted from the back of the room. "They're going to be here for months?"

But Principal Franco ignored the comment and went on to tell us about the arrangements that were being made. The cafeteria was going to be divided up into classrooms for the Rats, and we were going to be eating our lunches in our classrooms instead. The kindergarten classes were going to be doubling up so the R.R. Reginald kindergarten kids could have half their rooms, and we were all going to have to be courteous about sharing the yard at recess.

"The school board will fix the R.R. Reginald building as fast as they can," said Principal Franco. "But depending on how that goes, the R.R. Reginald students could be with us from as little as a month to as long as the remainder of the term."

I wanted to cry. And scream. And scream and cry. And judging from the shocked and outraged faces of the kids sitting around me, I wasn't the only one feeling that way.

Principal Franco was always telling us to have pride in our school and to think of it like a second home—and we did! There was hardly ever any litter in the school yard or fights at recess for exactly that reason. At Gledhill, we were good kids with good attitudes. But with the R.R. Reginald Rats invading, our school was sure to get totally ruined.

A typical Gledhill kid:

Normal hair

Bright eyes

Happy smile

Holding a book, for reading

A typical Reginald kid:

Shifty eyes

Wild hair

Smirky smile

Holding a balloon, for partying

And the worst part was, Principal Franco had made all kinds of plans without even asking us first!

"This is so unfair!" Don said, echoing my thoughts.

Bradley shook his head sadly. "We can't let them take over our school," he said.

"We don't even get a say," I wailed. "As usual, the adults just go ahead and decide things without even asking how we feel."

"Not this time," Bradley said, giving me a look that said it all. Then he added under his breath, "Right, Super Clara?"

It took me a split second to realize what he meant, but once I did, my whole outlook on the situation changed.

"Right," I said, trying to sound more confident than I felt, for Bradley's sake.

I had no idea how I was supposed to defend an entire school *and* keep Momo from moving away when it took all my concentration just to burn out a lightbulb...but maybe Bradley was right. Maybe if I just believed in myself and trained hard enough?

Who better to stop an invasion of rats than the world's most heroic computerized cat (and her humble creator)?

Those rotten rodents better run!

After all, Momo was one of my two best friends—and now the fate of my school was at stake, too. I couldn't afford to let doubt get in the way.

Raisin Power!

The situation was serious and there was no time to lose. Bradley and I started superhero training at first recess. We chose a picnic table near the fence where we'd have some privacy.

"So," Bradley said, putting down his giant envelope and handing me a piece of paper with a big chart on it. It was filled with huge words. He pointed to the top category. "According to realsuperpowers.org, your ability to spill hot-dog water and glasses of milk could be hydrokinesis—which is the power to control liquids. *But* it could also be telekinesis—the power to move things with your mind. I was thinking about it last night. The pinecone in the chocolate milk. And what about that time last Christmas, when we were in your living room and the tinsel floated off the tree and right across the room. Remember? There were three pieces in a row and we thought it was so freaky!

You must have had something to do with that."

I had *completely* forgotten about the flying tinsel. But now that he mentioned it, it *did* seem kind of super.

"And if all those things are related," Bradley went on with confidence, "then your powers could already be a lot stronger than we realize. All you have to do is learn to control them. That's where training comes in."

TOP 10 SUPERHERO QUALITIES

1. Has extraordinary powers
2. Is brave
3. Is strong
4. Is intelligent
5. Has thirst for justice
6. Has an unshakable sense of right and wrong
7. Is idealistic
8. Has an air of mystery
9. Is honorable
10. Is humble

A red ball with stars on it rolled up and hit our picnic table. "Over here!" Eric called. Eric, Jehan, Aubrey, and Siu were playing wall ball on the wall-ball-wall directly opposite from us. I picked up the ball and threw it back, then glanced over at them and motioned for Bradley to keep his voice down. We couldn't afford to have anyone overhear us. If word about my powers got out, I'd never develop an air of mystery!

Bradley nodded, then he slid the papers back into the envelope and reached into his coat pocket.

When most people think of superhero training, I'm pretty sure they envision cool stuff like light sabers, invisibility goggles, or at least a pair of awesome antigravity boots. But Bradley, apparently, had smaller ideas.

Three totally regular raisins

"Raisins?" I said. What did he think I was? A chinchilla?

"According to realsuperpowers.org, your mind is like a muscle. You have to start slow and build up. Otherwise you'll strain yourself."

He shook three raisins out of the box and lined them up on the picnic table. "Try to visualize them moving, okay? See your thoughts as waves of energy."

"Do I close my eyes or leave them open?" I asked.

Bradley shrugged. "The website didn't say. What did you do with the tinsel? And the pinecone?"

"They were definitely open. Except I don't know…I didn't even know I was doing it, so I wasn't really thinking about it."

"Good. Don't think about it this time, either."

I stared at the raisins. How was I supposed to visualize them moving if I wasn't thinking about it?

"This is *so* not working," I complained after a grand total of twenty seconds.

"Try harder," Bradley urged.

So I did, tilting my head every now and then to stare at the raisins from a slightly different angle. It was no use.

"Hey," Bradley said cheerfully. "Don't worry. Everyone with super powers must go through this. If it were easy, we'd *all* be moving stuff with our minds." He had a point. "Take a break. Tell me a joke or something."

"I'm too depressed to think of a joke right now," I replied miserably.

"Okay, I'll tell you one, then. Knock-knock."

"Who's there?"

"Ummm…cucumber."

"Cucumber who?"

Bradley shrugged. "I don't know."

"What do you mean you don't know?"

"I forgot to think of that part before I started."

"You mean the punch line?" I asked. "If you don't have a punch line, it's not a joke."

"Sure it is," Bradley said. "It's the beginning of a joke, anyway."

"Yeah, but it's not funny," I countered.

"It's *kind of funny*," he answered. "I mean, just the fact that a cucumber is knocking on a door."

I sighed. Sometimes Bradley could be totally exasperating! I was about to explain to him the basic structure of a joke (setup, buildup, punch line), but just then—

"Point!" I heard Eric yell.

The star ball bounced off the wall and rolled toward us again, disappearing underneath our table.

"Sorry," Eric said, coming over to get it this time.

I bent down to get the ball for him and put it into his outstretched hand.

"I don't know if you guys heard yet," he said, "but the fourth-graders are having a meeting by the monkey bars at second recess. We need to stake out our claim before the Rats get here. You know, decide which parts of the school yard are going to be off limits to them."

"We'll be there," I promised. After all, it was always good to be prepared…especially since I couldn't even seem to move a raisin with my mind, and it was looking less and less likely that we'd find some way to stop the Rats from coming.

"Clara!" Bradley whispered fiercely as Eric walked away. He tugged on my sleeve. "Look!" He motioned toward the picnic table with his head.

At first I didn't get what he was talking about—it was just the picnic table, still with three raisins on it. But then I saw it. Before, all three raisins had been in a straight line, but now one of them was all on its own, about half an inch away.

"Did we knock the table?" I asked.

Bradley shook his head. "I didn't touch it. Did you?"

I hadn't.

"Do you think you moved it with your mind?" he whispered.

I shrugged. "But I wasn't even trying," I said.

"Exactly! The same way you weren't even trying the other times. Plus," he said, with an "aha" look in his eye, "you were mad at me."

"No, I wasn't."

"Yes, you were. Just a little bit. About the cucumber joke."

Okay, maybe I had been slightly irritated, but I didn't see what that had to do with anything.

"Think about yesterday at the track meet. Right before the hot-dog water tipped, you were really mad at Becky about the Gator," he explained.

"Maybe," I said, still feeling uncertain. But then I remembered…when my milk had spilled at dinner, I'd also been mad—that time at my parents, for pretending that everything was fine even though Momo was moving.

"And then with the tinsel," he went on. "Remember? Your dad called us chicken legs." He grinned.

It was true! Bradley and I had been lying on our backs on the carpet in front of my Christmas tree, our feet pressed together, having a leg-wrestling match. My dad had called us both "chicken legs" right before he went out the door to hang the Christmas lights he'd programmed to flash in time to "Rudolph the Red-Nosed Reindeer." I was furious. And then the tinsel had magically floated through the air.

"And now you were a little bit mad at me, and the raisin moved a little bit. So that's it!" Bradley exclaimed. "All you have to do is think about the thing you want to move, but at the same time not think about it, and then get as mad as possible!"

He was right. I couldn't believe I hadn't realized it sooner. I mean, it was so OBVIOUS! Not to mention, it was the exact same way that @Cat harnessed her most impressive powers. The more I thought about it, the more it was like I'd known all along, in some small way.

Repulsor beams!

How dare you scare the postman away! My catnip has been on backorder for WEEKS!

@CAT harnesses her rage to shoot her billion-megawatt repulsor beams @ Poodle Noodle.

THE END

I grabbed the box of raisins off the table, shook some into my hand, and popped them into my mouth. I chewed them thoughtfully, getting a faraway look in my eye like superheroes sometimes do.

I gazed out over the school yard at the rusty monkey bars and babyish climber, much like @Cat might gaze out over the rolling hills of the land of Animalea.

"I think you're on to something, Bradley," I said, gaining confidence with each passing second. "You just wait and see! I'm going to defend Gledhill Elementary to the bitter end, if it's the last thing I do."

While Mrs. Smith went over spelling words and talked about the water cycle that afternoon, I put my mind to work on a plan to ward off the R.R. Reginald Rats. I made a huge list in my notebook, but most of the things I came up with were just a touch too evil.

Super Clara's Possible Plans to Ward Off the Rats

- **USING MY POWER TO SPILL THINGS:**
I can set up a lemonade stand and sell poisonous lemonade to the R.R. Reginald kids. I could spill some on them, to be extra mean. (Possible Problems: Lemonade is sticky. Might attract ants. Also, what if the Gledhill kids accidentally drink some? Plus, it's not a good idea to poison anyone, even if they have bad attitudes.)

- **USING THE POWER TO MOVE THINGS WITH MY MIND:**
I can make all the R.R. Reginald kids' stuff float around so that they feel like they're learning in zero gravity and it just gets annoying and then they leave. (Possible Problems: People might get hit in the head with textbooks and staplers. Also, antigravity might actually be fun, and then they'd only want to stay.)

- **USING MY SUPERSONIC HEARING:**
I can listen in to all the Rats' secrets and then spread gossip about them until they get so sad they just leave. (Possible Problems: Gossiping is mean. @Cat would never stoop so low, and neither will I!)

- **USING MY CHINCHILLA TELEPATHY:**
I can...I don't even know.

- **USING MY POWER TO WAKE UP AT 7:14! EXACTLY!**
I'm pretty sure I'll *never* think of any way to make that useful.

I laid my head down on my desk and let out a quiet sigh. Moving a raisin was one thing, and I was sure I could build my powers if I tried hard, but would it be enough? If I was going to get rid of the Rats, I'd need something really impressive. A power that could not be stopped!

"This is your list of spelling words for next week," Mrs. Smith said. She walked to the front of each row and handed the first person a pile of papers.

"No," I muttered under my breath. "No, no, no. Not homework. No homework." I had so much superhero training to do, and a big list of Mrs. Smith's impossible spelling words was the last thing I needed! Not that I *ever* really needed it. The week before, for example, the first spelling word was "consistent." I ask you! Will I ever need that word in my entire life? It means "the same" so why not just say "the same"?

Aubrey passed back the stack of papers and I groaned. That week's first word was "tongue." Honestly?!

"It's so unfair. Couldn't we for once not have homework?" I muttered to myself, folding the sheet and stuffing it into the pocket in my planner.

If @Cat were in charge of spelling test words, the world would be a better place.

Mrs. Smith was busy writing the reminder about Monday's spelling test on the board, and all of a sudden, she stopped, her chalk midway through the letter *P*.

"Actually, you know what? I think we're going to put our spelling test off until later in the week." She picked up the eraser and rubbed the letters out. "No homework this weekend. Just enjoy yourselves."

I nearly jumped up and cheered—and I wasn't the only one.

"And be sure to give the notice about the situation with R.R. Reginald to your parents," Mrs. Smith reminded us. But in light of what had just happened, even *that* didn't get my spirits down.

"Holy cheese. I can't believe Mrs. Smith didn't give us a single bit of homework this weekend. No spelling study words. Not even math problems!" Bradley said as we put our coats on. "When's the last time *that* happened?"

"Bradley," I said, glancing around to make sure nobody was listening in, then staring straight into his eyes. "It didn't just happen. Is there a word— like hydrokinesis or electrokinesis—for getting other people to do exactly what you want them to do? Like getting your teacher to cancel all the homework and postpone all the tests?"

"Mind control?" he said, his eyes going as big as satellite dishes.

"Bradley," I whispered, "I think this might be so much bigger than raisins."

"Holy cheese," he said again. "Is it ever."

An Oscar-Worthy Performance

That afternoon when the school bus pulled up at our stop, Momo was waiting for me. She was standing beside Svetlana—and I knew exactly why she was there. I'd seen the For Sale sign on her lawn from the bus window when we went past. It had that lady with the very white teeth and very big hair on it—the same one who seemed to sell all the houses in our neighborhood. Above her

picture there was a sign that read, "Coming soon." It meant that Momo was about to break her terrible news to me. Under any other circumstances, I would have felt like crying, but for a girl who'd just learned she has the power of mind control (in addition to the power to spill things, move things with her mind, burn out lightbulbs and batteries, wake up at 7:14 exactly, *and* communicate with chinchillas), a little For Sale sign didn't seem like much of a match.

"Hello, darlings!" Svetlana squished Bradley and Val to her chest, then smooched them all over, leaving lipstick on their faces.

Bradley winced and I tried to look away out of respect. Unfortunately that meant I spotted Pete Murphy laughing at Bradley while making fish lips against the glass at the back of the bus. I glared at him, trying to see if I had the power to freeze people's faces in time. It was hard to tell if it worked, though, because the bus was already turning the corner.

"Hi, brat," Momo said, ruffling my hair. "Good day?"

"The best," I answered, giving her a huge smile. "And to top it all off, no homework this weekend. Hey…" I said, staring down the street past the twisty branches of the terrible tree.

One of the scary birds caught me looking. "BA-CAW!" it croaked, making me jump.

I quickly turned back to Momo. "What's that on your lawn?" I asked.

Momo sighed sadly. "That," she said, "is something you and I need to talk about. Over ice cream. I already told your dad we're going. Thirty-one flavors!" she said. "How many left?"

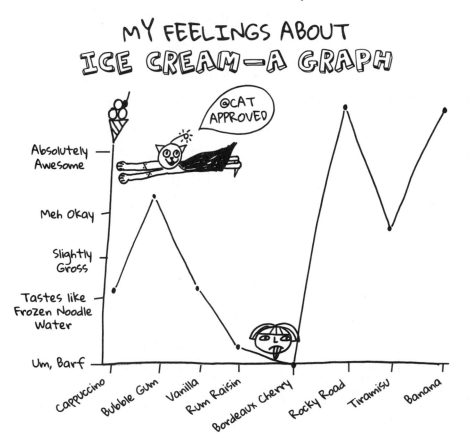

MY FEELINGS ABOUT
ICE CREAM—A GRAPH

@CAT APPROVED

Absolutely Awesome

Meh Okay

Slightly Gross

Tastes like Frozen Noodle Water

Um, Barf

Cappuccino   Bubble Gum   Vanilla   Rum Raisin   Bordeaux Cherry   Rocky Road   Tiramisu   Banana

Momo and I had been working for months to try every single flavor at Baskin-Robbins. Some of them were pretty disgusting (like Bordeaux Cherry), but we were soldiering on anyway.

"Seventeen," I said, "not counting the frozen yogurt." (Because, really, who counts the frozen yogurt?)

"Ay, Chihuahua," Momo said, waving good-bye to Bradley, Val, and Svetlana. "Come on. We've got work to do."

Now, I'm not claiming to be some kind of movie star, but I *did* give a pretty impressive performance. I was two licks into a cone of Chocolate Brownie Overload when Momo started telling me about the retirement home far, far away and the open house she'd be having the next weekend to try to sell her place. I let my mouth drop open, then acted like I was too shocked and upset to even eat. That's called being "in character." Normally, I *love* anything with chocolate.

"But...but...but," I stammered, which I thought was a nice touch. "When will I get to see you?"

"You can come up any weekend you want. They've got nature trails. And a pool. Not to mention a huge stash of board games in the common room."

I sniffed once, then licked the back of my hand, which was getting covered in ice cream drips.

"Let me get you a napkin," Momo said. I kept acting sniffly and devastated, but the second she turned her back at the spoon-and-napkin stand, I stared hard into the back of her skull, controlling her brain waves like this:

DON'T MOVE...

DON'T MOVE...

MOVING IS STUPID...

DON'T MOVE...

And I think it kind of worked, because when she sat down—

"I'm going to miss you more than I think I can stand," she said, then put a napkin down in front of me. "I don't *really* want to go, you know."

I nearly jumped up and cheered. Ha! See? My mind control powers were already unstoppable!

"But I know it's time," she went on. "I'm not getting any younger. And you're getting older, too."

I didn't see what *that* had to do with anything.

"In a few years, you'll be a teenager, Clara," Momo explained. "You might not want to spend so much of your free time with an old lady anymore."

"I'm *not* going to be a teenager!" I said. It was true. I'd already decided. Or at least I'd decided never to act like one. I'd watched my cousin Tony do it and it didn't look like *any* fun. From what I could tell, it involved a bit of eye rolling, a lot of looking bored, and way too many black clothes.

"And I'm *always* going to want to spend my free time with you," I added.

Momo looked out the window and smiled like she didn't quite believe me. After a minute, she reached across the table and took my still-sticky hand in hers.

"I promise you, brat, we're both going to get through this just fine."

But her eyes clouded over with tears when she said it, and I knew it wasn't true. Thankfully I also knew it wasn't actually going to happen. Okay, so maybe I hadn't completely mind-controlled her *just yet*, but the open house was a whole week away and I *wasn't* going to give up.

"I know this is hard, but I need your support," she said. "Because I'm having a hard enough time with the idea myself."

"Okay," I lied, looking her right in the eye. "I'll support you. Except I want to spend every single last bit of time with you. Maybe I can help you with stuff? You know, to get the house ready?"

My aunt had sold her house the year before, so I knew that to convince people to buy your place, you had to make it look like something from a decorating magazine, with your shoes lined up straight and no hair in the sink.

"Thank you, Clara," Momo said. "What a nice offer."

She was right. It was *really* nice of me, even though I was mostly doing it so I could stay nearby and manipulate her brain waves.

"Maybe Bradley can help, too," I suggested. "I mean, you don't have much time. So the more help, the better, right?"

"That would be nice," Momo said.

I smiled, but not too much (I was still in character). With Bradley by my side and my powers growing stronger every minute, I had no doubt Momo and I would have all the time we needed to try the remaining sixteen ice cream flavors, and then start all over again if we wanted to.

The next morning was Saturday, but of course I still woke up at 7:14, exactly! I ate some toast and went straight to Momo's. I let myself in through the back door and stepped around a stack of cardboard boxes. By the looks of things, Momo had already been hard at work preparing for the open house the next weekend.

The shelf she usually stacked old newspapers on was empty and her funny teapot collection, which normally lined the top of the kitchen cabinets, was almost all packed away. The only one left was the fat chef teapot, where the lid is the chef's hat and tea pours out his arm. It's usually my favorite, but on that day, Fat Chef looked sad and lonely up there without his neighbors, Yellow Polka Dot pot, Rooster teapot, and Kitty Cat cream-and-sugar set.

"Momo!" I called, but there was no answer and I could hear the faint sound of the shower running upstairs. I went to the front window and sat down beside Fatty-Fatty-Two-Tip—Momo's enormous orange cat—who was lounging in his itty-bitty basket in the sun.

Purr, I commanded him silently with my thoughts. And he did. Loudly. Which was a relief.

The night before, Bradley and I had done some more superhero training in his backyard, and it hadn't gone so great. We'd started by filling up a few flowerpots from his shed with hose water and seeing if I could spill them.

I couldn't.

Next I'd tried to levitate some leaves, which worked a little bit, but it was hard to tell what was due to my awesome brain power and what was just the wind. Finally I'd tried to mind-control

Bradley—like a silent game of Simon Says.

Stand on your head, I commanded him with my mind.

He spun around.

Bark like a dog.

He stood on one foot.

"Why isn't anything working!?" I sighed.

Bradley didn't seem worried. "Maybe it's too noisy back here, and you can't concentrate." The neighbors in the next yard were fixing their shed, and with all the hammering, it was hard to focus. "Or maybe you're just tired," he went on. "You burned out a lightbulb, levitated a raisin, *and* mind-controlled a teacher. That's a lot of super work for one day when you're just getting started."

He was probably right. Actually, I thought, he was definitely right. I rubbed Fatty-Fatty's white-tipped ears and listened to him purr. A good night's sleep and a chance to rest my mind was basically all I'd needed. And it was a lucky thing, because I had some serious work to do. Not all of it was super, either. Getting a house ready for sale involved a lot of scrubbing and painting and moving stuff around.

"Thank goodness you kids are here to help," Momo said when she finally came down from the shower. She had a kerchief tied around her head with bits of wet hair sticking out. Bradley had arrived by then, too, so Momo set out two mugs of hot chocolate for us and tea for herself. She pulled a list out of her pocket. "I'll start by taking down some pictures and touching up the paint. Bradley, maybe you can sweep and wash the floors. Clara, you're on windows, okay? We want them streak-free to let in lots of light."

Momo put on our favorite CD—*Dance Hits of the '60s*—and as we bop-shoo-bopped to the "Peppermint Twist," I stuck as close to her as possible so I could send a steady stream of "do not move" vibes with my mind.

It was NOT as easy as it sounds. I don't mean the vibe-sending. That part was fine. Keeping up with Momo was the problem. First she went to the attic storage space to get some cans of paint, which she set on a tarp on the dining room table. While she was doing that, she noticed a burned-out bulb in the chandelier. (Don't look at me! I didn't do it!) She thought she had a replacement in the hall closet, but when she got there, she remembered they were actually under the kitchen sink. Then, when she opened the cabinet to get a new bulb, she noticed how messy it was, so she piled all the old cleaning brushes and shoe polish containers into a box and lugged them up to the attic. There she found two lamps that she thought would look great in the living room, so she brought them downstairs, only to discover *those* bulbs were burned out, so it was back to the kitchen.

By the time we'd made it back to the dining room, where the paint was waiting, I was out of breath, not to mention out of excuses for why I needed to be *exactly* where Momo was at all times. The kitchen was easy (I needed a drink of water), and the living room wasn't so hard (it had a window, and I was supposed to be washing windows—even though I hadn't actually started). But the attic was a little harder.

Still, my hard work seemed to be paying off. "Lord, love a duck! This is a big job," Momo said as she pried the lids off all the different colors of paint. There was sky blue for touch-ups in the bathroom, pink for Momo's bedroom, minty green for the dining room. The colors reminded me of the marshmallows inside a box of Lucky Charms cereal. "If this is just getting the place ready for sale," she went on, "I hate to think what actually moving is going to be like."

"It's true," I said, squirting my first squirt of water and vinegar onto the dining room window. "Moving is *super* stressful. When my aunt Tammy moved last year, she said it almost *killed her*." I emphasized the last part to show how serious it was.

HERE LIES
TAMMY HUMBLE
WHO DIED OF REAL-ESTATE- RELATED CAUSES. MAY SHE REST IN PEACE AND NEVER MOVE AGAIN.

Momo sighed, then poured some sky-blue paint into a tray. "I guess I'll get started on the bathroom now," she said. "Call me if you need anything."

The bathroom! My mind was already racing, trying to think of what possible excuse (besides the obvious) I could make for absolutely needing to be in the bathroom while Momo was painting, but just then, the phone rang.

"Oh! That'll be the real estate agent." Momo set the paint tray down and went into the kitchen. I was about to follow her, but she motioned for me to wait. "Why don't you keep on with those windows, Clara? And then maybe you can help Bradley with the floors. If we finish before lunch, I'll take you both out for ice cream. Sixteen flavors to go."

Bradley grinned and started to mop faster. Meanwhile I squeaked my paper towel back and forth across the window, not even bothering to think about whether I'd get Fudge Ripple or Birthday Cake Bonanza.

From where I was standing, I could hear Momo's voice in the kitchen.

"Hi, Susan. Yes. We're still on track for the open house next weekend, but it's going to be tight.

There are so many little jobs. Plus, out of nowhere, the dishwasher broke last night. I'll have to get that fixed now."

I squirted more vinegar water on the window and watched it dribble down the glass like tears. *We're still on track for the open house?* So much for my mind control!

I put the roll of paper towels down and stared hard at Bradley's bucket full of floor-washing water. "Spill!" I whispered at it. It didn't budge. "Spill!" I said again, raising my hands over my head and getting as angry as I could, which was pretty angry, let me tell you. I mean, what good were super powers if you couldn't even count on them to work when you needed them?

Bradley stopped mopping and gave me his most encouraging look.

"Spill, water! I command you!" I hissed, screwing up my entire face in concentration. Not even a drop spilled, but my scary whispering *did* manage to wake Fatty-Fatty-Two-Tip, who hopped out of his basket and started to lumber toward the safety of the kitchen, looking back over his shoulder to keep an eye on me.

"As soon as we're done here, I'll give you a call so you can schedule the house stager," I heard Momo say to the agent. "Absolutely. The cats and I will stay at my sister's place during the open house. That's right," Momo said. "I'll take the litter boxes, too. I know buyers can be put off by the smell of animals."

I raised my arms one more time. "Spill!" I commanded the bucket, but it was no use.

"It's okay," Bradley whispered. "Just take a break. *And believe in yourself.* The powers will come to you."

I was starting to doubt that. I picked up my roll of paper towels and headed for the mirror over the fireplace mantle. It was covered in dust. "Some superhero," I muttered, squirting my reflection in the face with vinegar and water. "I can't even spill things anymore!"

Then—all of a sudden—*SPLOOSH!* CRASH!

"Fatty-Fatty, look out!" Bradley shouted. I barely had time to turn around to see what the commotion was before it all happened.

Bradley's wash bucket had tipped sideways, sending a river of soapy water across the floor just as Fatty-Fatty-Two-Tip—who had been so cruelly disturbed from his slumber—was trying to cross the dining room to get to the kitchen.

When the water hit his paws, he defied the law of gravity. The twenty-pound cat leapt nearly straight up into the air. I could tell he was hoping to make it to safety on the dining room table. And he almost did. His front paws landed on the drop cloth Momo had put down to protect the table and he dug into it with his claws, but his back paws fell short. He paddled at the air with them furiously.

But it was no use.

Fatty-Fatty was going down.

And the tarp was coming with him.

And with the tarp came the paint.

First Momo's paint tray then three cans toppled sideways and thudded to the ground, oozing marshmallow-colored paint like slow rivers into the surging sea of dirty floor water.

"What on earth?" Momo said, peering in from the kitchen.

Fatty-Fatty, who was stuck like a turtle on his back, wiggled his body furiously and finally managed to flip over. He ran up the stairs, leaving a trail of pastel footprints behind him.

"It spilled—!" I whispered in shock.

Bradley nodded.

"But I wasn't even looking at it!"

"The mirror," he whispered back. "You were looking in the mirror. And you were mad and frustrated, but not trying too hard. That's the key, remember? Your powers must have bounced off the mirror and hit the bucket of water!"

"Are you sure?" I said.

"Of course I'm sure," he answered.

"Susan," Momo said into the phone, "I'm going to have to call you back. We've just had a minor disaster." She hung up and stepped into the living room. "Oh, good lord," she said, putting a hand over her mouth.

Bradley started mopping, and Momo went to get some rags. Meanwhile I just stood there, taking in the devastation.

Momo sighed when she got back. "First the dishwasher, and now this?" She stood for a while in the doorway with some old tea towels, then looked up to the heavens (or more accurately, the ceiling). "Is this supposed to be some kind of sign?"

\\\

Even though Bradley was mopping as fast as he could, the water and paint were still oozing across the floor, spreading in all directions like a melted rainbow. It was beautiful, in a way. But was it a sign? Well, it all depended on if you believed in that kind of thing, I guess…

@Cat projecting a rainbow force field into the sky to protect Animalea from sadness.

Overrun by Rodents

On Monday morning, the R.R. Reginald kids arrived, bringing their bad attitudes and mean principal with them—not to mention their cranky parents.

"Well, this is just great," said one mother, who was wearing a shaggy fur coat. "How are we supposed to know where the kids line up? There was no communication. None at all!"

"Tell me about it," said another. "This is total chaos."

That much was true. Our school yard, which was usually filled with pleasant, chatting parents and happy, playing children, was overrun with unruly rats. They were sprawled on the benches, hanging upside down from the monkey bars, and crowded onto the climber like it was a sinking ship.

"This is worse than I'd feared," I said to Bradley, who nodded somberly.

I put my hands up against my temples to help myself concentrate.

Go away! I tried to mind-control a group of shrieking R.R. Reginald kids. *Go invade some other school!* I shifted my focus to the mother in the fur coat. *Leave now!*

Fur Coat Mom glanced at her watch. "I'm going to be late for work," she said to the mom beside her. "Would you mind watching Abby to make sure she gets in safely?"

Ha! Okay, so maybe that wasn't *exactly* the kind of leaving I'd wanted her to do, but it was pretty close. My powers were definitely getting stronger. Now if I could just keep my focus!

"Why are you squishing your own head?"

Unfortunately, the fake-friendly voice of Bossy Becky McDougall made intense focus all but impossible. I dropped my hands from my temples and turned to face her.

"Because the kids from your school are giving me a headache," I lied. "Are you guys always this loud?"

"Are you guys *always* this rude to your guests?" she shot back.

Guests? They were more like invaders!

"Don't get too comfortable here," I answered. "You *won't* be staying long."

"Yeah, we hope not," Becky said, glancing at Darla and Joanna, who were standing behind her in their usual places wearing their usual smirks. "I can tell just from the school yard that this place is the worst. Are those monkey bars a hundred years old or something?"

They *were* a hundred years old. At least. In fact, it was possible that our monkey bars had been around since before monkeys evolved into humans. But she didn't have any right to say so. This wasn't her school!

"You'd better watch what you say about Gledhill," I informed her.

"Or else what?" she challenged.

Or else I'll levitate your school bag up into the air and dump everything in it out on your head…or mind-control your brain so you get all the answers wrong and get *F*s on your tests…or spill something all over the floor right in front of you so that when you go walking past in your stupid silver running shoes, you'll fall right down and everyone will go *ha, ha, HA*. I wanted to say all those things…but of course, I couldn't, so instead I said this:

"Or else I'll tell our principal on you." Okay, so it wasn't the most brilliant comeback in the history of ever, but I was under a lot of pressure.

"Ooooooooh. I'm *soooooooo* scared," Becky said. "If you do that, I'll just tell *our* principal on *you*. And trust me, she's way scarier."

I could already tell. Even though she was all the way across the yard, we could hear the R.R. Reginald principal—Principal Demerit—yelling at a kid who had just dropped a granola bar wrapper on the ground. Principal Demerit was about six feet tall with broad shoulders, long black hair, and a stick-straight way of standing that made it clear you didn't want to mess with her. Not even a little.

The Grand High Rat (a.k.a. Principal Demerit) on garbage patrol.

I want this picked up YESTERDAY! Move, people, MOVE!

Tiny piece of lint on the floor

"See ya," Becky said dismissively. Then she flipped her hair and walked away, with her two friends following close behind.

"Arrrrrgghhh!" I said as soon as she was gone. "She annoys me *so* much."

"I know," Bradley said. "Just avoid her, okay? As much as you can…at least until we can get them to leave," he added under his breath.

Avoiding Becky was good advice. It was completely what I would have done, too, if Coach Shipley hadn't made it impossible.

I'd been looking forward to track and field practice all weekend. Besides baking some not-so-delicious spelt muffins, my mom had bought me a cool precision digital stopwatch to celebrate my blue-ribbon win, and I was dying to show it off.

But when we got out to the field at lunch, I forgot all about its memory function and countdown timer because there, lounging on the grass, was a pack of Rats.

"What are you doing here?" Eric said, giving them a dirty look.

"Umm…having track practice," Joanna answered. "Our coach told us to meet here."

"Well, this is our track time," Angela said, putting her hands on her hips. "You guys are going to have to find another field. Or else come back later."

"Look," Eric said. "Coach Shipley is coming. She'll tell them to get lost." We waited expectantly as our coach came across the field with her clipboard in hand.

"Hello, Gledhill Gators!" she called out.

"HELLO, COACH!" we yelled together, using our most enthusiastic yells, because being enthusiastic is what we do best.

"And hello, R.R. Reginald Raccoons!" she added.

Some of the R.R. Reginald kids kind of grunted, and one sort of half-waved while she took a sip from her water bottle.

"I'm glad to see everyone's here," our coach went

on. "Coach Donahue is feeling a little under the weather and had to head home, so I offered to coach both teams today."

Coach Shipley didn't miss the fact that nobody looked *at all* happy about the arrangement.

"I know there was some bad blood at the semifinals last week, but I want us to look at this as an opportunity to put that behind us. Line up, everyone! Gators on one side and Raccoons on the other. We're all going to shake hands."

So we did, but none of us liked it, and when it was my turn to shake Becky's hand, she squeezed it so tightly that she nearly broke it. Plus John Connolly (the R.R. Reginald long-distance-running champion) had such a wet palm that I swear he must have spat on it first. We were going to be lucky if none of us caught the plague.

Finally, with that unpleasantness behind us, it was time to start training—and that ended up being even worse.

We started with two laps around the track. The Rats kept trying to trip us whenever Coach Shipley wasn't looking. Then we moved on to one-footed jump rope with five-second intervals on each foot. Becky "accidentally" hit me in the back of the head with her jump rope twice. Next we did some triceps and quadriceps stretches. This time, at least, I managed to position myself far enough away from Becky that I could ignore her—well, mostly. That got harder to do when an ant crawled onto her leg and she started screaming.

GREAT BIG SCREAM

AHHH!

Teeny tiny ant

"Good job, everyone," Coach Shipley said after we'd finished the drills and she'd had a little talk with Becky about her overreaction to ants. "Let's move on to running long jump. Why don't we have a friendly competition to see who can jump the farthest?" she suggested. "The Gators or the

Raccoons? Kelly, can you help me measure and add up the scores?"

"Did you see how Becky hit me in the head with her skipping rope?" I said to Bradley as our teammate Kelly went to get the measuring stick and the rest of us went to line up.

"The big guy in the blue shirt tripped me twice on the track," Bradley complained, rubbing a bruise on his shin that was already getting purple.

"I always knew they were evil," Eric added. "Dealing with them at track meets is bad enough, but it's even worse in our own school!"

Eric was right, of course. And I knew I had to do something. I'd been mind-controlling them every chance I got, but it didn't seem to be working yet. What else could I possibly do to get rid of them?

"Oh, my God!" I heard Becky say as she walked over to join the line a few spots behind Bradley and me. "I just had *another* ant on me. What's *wrong* with this place? It's covered in bugs."

And that was when it occurred to me: if I couldn't mind-control them into leaving, then maybe I could scare them into it. As I got closer to the front of the line, I craned my neck to get a good look at the sand pit, estimating the spot I'd need to land on. Finally, it was my turn.

"Go, Clara!" my teammates yelled as I raced down the yard. I reached the white line, launched myself with my left foot using all my strength, and flew through the air. To make my plan work, I needed all the distance I could get.

"Way to go!" Bradley said. He'd gone right before me, so he was standing near the sand pit. That was key to my plan, too.

"Quick!" I panted. "Pass me my water bottle."

He passed it, then I bent down, acting as if I were tying my shoe while Kelly rolled out the tape measure.

"One point seven meters!" she called out. It was the longest jump anyone had done yet!

"Good job, Clara! Clear the pit, please," Coach Shipley yelled.

"One second," I said over my shoulder. "I just need to finish tying my shoelace."

"You can step outside the pit to do that," she called back, but I pretended I didn't hear. "Clara, I don't want to ask you again," she yelled. "Other students are waiting their turn."

Satisfied that I'd finished my work, I stood up, quickly kicking some dry sand around.

"Sorry," I yelled, then I stepped out of the pit and stood close by, waiting to see if my plan would work—and did it ever! Well...eventually.

Becky, Joanna, Darla, and two other Rats finished their jumps, and it wasn't until the guy in blue who'd tripped Bradley (whose name, it turns out, was Rick) had his turn that things got interesting.

"YES!" he boomed when he landed. He looked back over his shoulder at the distance. "Make sure you measure right," he said to Kelly, keeping his feet planted so she wouldn't miss a single millimeter. "Start right at the line."

When he found out he'd beaten my record by a full ten centimeters, he started doing a victory dance.

Turns out that was a bad idea. Especially because the ants were already pretty mad about the water I'd poured into their home. They'd been coming up out of the hole in a steady stream ever since.

"Rick! Your shoe!" Becky shrieked. "It's covered in ants!"

It definitely was—and they were already starting the trek up his tree trunk of a shin.

"Aaaaack!" He started to shriek and hop around, swatting at his leg. "There are millions of them! Get them off! Somebody help

Important Life Lesson: Never do a victory dance on an anthill.

This tree smells WEIRD, Frank!

Not very leafy either!

me." But like typical Rats, his teammates only seemed interested in their own well-being. Nobody stepped in to help him until Coach Shipley finally took pity.

"Brush them off. There you go," she said calmly. But there really were millions—or at least hundreds—and it looked like it was going to take a while.

"Clara?" Bradley whispered, eyeing me suspiciously. "Did you have anything to do with that?"

I smiled. Bradley and I had done an archeological dig in that sand pit at one recess not too long before, and we'd made the mistake of disturbing the very same giant anthill. We weren't such babies about it, though. I mean, they were only ants.

"I think they're in my underpants now!" Rick squealed, hopping around some more.

Okay, so maybe it hadn't exactly been a *super* move, but it was pretty inspired, not to mention a good use of previous knowledge.

"A superhero knows how to think on her feet," I said to Bradley, "and use her head."

I'm feeling a little dizzy, Poodle Noodle, but I will still DEFEAT YOU!!!

The time @CAT tried to think on her head and use her feet. It wasn't her finest moment.

"Super Clara," he said, putting an arm around my shoulder as we watched Coach Shipley escort Rick and his ant-filled underpants back to the school. "You are not to be trifled with."

Foiled by a Tissue

I spent the next four days doing some serious super work. I started by using my electrokinesis to mess with the lights in the cafeteria, which had been divided into classrooms for the Rats. I sat in class, scrunching up my face in concentration, thinking about the lights every chance I got—which made Mrs. Smith ask more than once if I needed the hall pass to go the bathroom.

The cafeteria is in the basement of the school. It has only a few windows and I thought that by plunging the Rats into near-total darkness, I could make them feel uneasy, even if they refused to be scared off completely.

"I can't believe the lights went off three different times this morning," I overheard Joanna complaining to Darla at recess.

"Tell me about it!" she whined back. "I was trying to sneak fruit snacks from inside my desk, and I accidentally almost ate one of my erasers."

"I'm not surprised the lights don't work. This school is so old and broken down," Joanna went on, wrinkling her nose. As if they had a right to talk about our school being broken down when their own school walls were filled with mold!

Next I spilled an entire tray of milk. Or I think I did. The lunch lady who was carrying it into the cafeteria for the Rats tripped, and there wasn't even anything much on the floor. Plus I was standing nearby, feeling angry about an R.R. Reginald kid who'd just pushed past me to get to the water fountain—so odds were good that I'd had something to do with it.

I even used my supersonic hearing to listen in on a conversation between one of the Rats—this pip-squeak of a fourth-grader called Abby— and Principal Demerit. It turned out they were only talking about a missing library book, and there wasn't anything I could really do with that information. But still, the girl had the quietest-ever voice (she was more like a mouse than a rat), and the fact that I'd heard what she said at all was pretty impressive.

@Cat demonstrating her supersonic hearing.

What's more (even though it was starting to get in the way of me paying attention in class), I kept up a steady stream of mind control, sending thoughts of leaving Gledhill in the direction of the cafeteria all day long.

"I don't get it!" I complained to Bradley that Saturday as we sat by my bedroom window. "I've been doing my best and it's *still* not working!" Bradley was busy trying to teach Bijou some new chinchilla tricks, while I was drawing and keeping an eye on Momo's house.

Despite the huge mess I'd made of her dining room floor with the paint and water—and even though she'd wondered out loud if it was some kind of sign that she shouldn't sell the house—it looked like she was going ahead with it anyway. The first open house was officially on, and about four families had been through so far.

I wasn't all that worried, of course. Even though I hadn't managed to get the R.R. Reginald kids to leave just yet, I had a pretty good track record for mind-controlling adults. If I could just make sure to be at the window whenever someone came to see the house, I was certain I could convince them not to buy it.

"I don't get it, either," Bradley said, holding up a raisin. "Kiss," he said, then he waited for Bijou to nuzzle his hand before giving it to her. "The mind control worked on Mrs. Smith, and on that mom in the school yard. And sometimes it works on Momo. There's no reason why it shouldn't work on kids, too. Unless…" He trailed off, getting an "I have an idea" look in his eyes.

"Unless what?" I asked, looking up from the new comic strip I was working on.

@CAT and BIJOU the BRAVE: TECH TROUBLE

"Unless it *is* working on them, but there's just nothing they can do about it…That's it, Clara! I think maybe you're mind-controlling the wrong people!"

I didn't quite get what he was saying. If I wasn't supposed to mind-control the kids, who was I supposed to mind-control? I wasn't able to ask him right away, either, because just then, my mom came in, holding the laundry basket under one arm.

"Clara? What's this?" she asked. She was holding out a handful of something white and shredded.

"Kleenex," I said, barely looking up from my work on @*Cat and Bijou the Brave: Tech Trouble*.

"I know it's Kleenex," my mom said. "I think my real question is, why didn't you take it out of your pocket before putting your clothes in the hamper?" My mom and I had this discussion pretty much once a week. Sometimes twice.

"I forgot," I said.

Just then, the garage door started to groan and shake the floor underneath us. My dad still hadn't managed to fix it. In fact, ever since he had "improved" it, every time a person walked past our house, the sensor got triggered and the garage door rattled open or closed.

At first the people across the street had complained about the noise, and my dad had promised to get to it as soon as he could, but at least in our family, we'd gotten used to ignoring it—the same way we ignored the drippy faucet in the basement bathroom and didn't mind how you had to jiggle your key in the front door lock a certain way to make it work. Anyway, my dad was pretty busy with his newest invention—a self-propelled, solar-powered lawn mower. He didn't have time to be worrying about garage doors, which was fine with me.

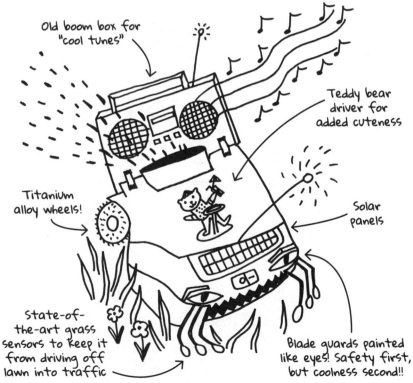

Old boom box for "cool tunes"

Teddy bear driver for added cuteness

Titanium alloy wheels!

Solar panels

State-of-the-art grass sensors to keep it from driving off lawn into traffic

Blade guards painted like eyes! Safety first, but coolness second!!

The garage-door-gone-haywire was kind of convenient, especially when I was trying to keep an eye on Momo's house to mind-control possible buyers. It was like an alarm that let Bradley and me know someone was coming. Bradley glanced out the window, then back at me urgently to let me know some new people had arrived.

"Clara. I've asked you this a hundred times," my mom went on, oblivious to the situation. "You *need* to remember to check your pockets. If you forget again, I'm going to have to ask you to start doing your own laundry."

"Okay, Mom. Sure. Sorry," I said, already starting toward the window.

But I should have known better. Taking "that tone" with my mom never works. It's like she has a small but real super power of her own. You can't fake an apology. If you aren't really, truly, down-on-your-knees sorry with a cherry on top, she'll know.

"Clara!" she said in her no-nonsense tone. "Are you really listening to me?"

"Yes, Mom," I said, stopping in my tracks and giving her my most serious, most responsible face. "I'll remember. I promise."

APOLOGY
ALERT!!!

REMORSE
RADAR

SUPER
MOM

I detect a child within a five-mile radius who is not truly sorry!

"And what about Bijou's cage? Have you cleaned it recently?"

"Ummm…I'll do it tonight."

"Clara!" She sighed. "Not tonight. Now. Bradley won't mind, will you, Bradley?"

He shook his head.

Really, I was getting off easy. Sometimes when I forget to clean Bijou's cage, my mom marches me over to the official chinchilla contract posted on my wall and makes me read subsection 1.3 out loud.

Still, even though my mom's lecture was short, it was much, much too long.

"Oh no!" Bradley put his head in his hands as soon as my mom closed the door. "You missed some people. It was a mom with really red hair and a boy about our age. They walked right into Momo's house while your mom was talking about Kleenex shreds."

"It's okay," I said. "I'll just get them on the way out, right? While we wait, tell me more about your theory. About mind-controlling the kids."

"Right," he said, picking up Bijou and setting her back in her cage. "What I meant is, maybe your mind control *is* working. The R.R. Reginald kids hate it at our school."

This was true. Since the second they'd arrived, all they'd done was complain about how old the building was, how lame our playground was, and how much they wanted to go back to their own school. "But they're not the ones who get to make the decisions, right?" he went on.

"Right," I said. "So I should mind-control their parents?"

Bradley shook his head.

"Their teachers?" I tried.

He shook his head again. "Think bigger."

"Their principal?!"

"Bingo!" he said.

I wasn't so sure about this new plan. Mind-controlling kids was one thing, but a principal? And not just any principal! The scariest principal in the history of principals! Then again, Bradley was probably right. Principal Demerit must have been the one who made the decision to relocate the R.R. Reginald kids to Gledhill while their school got fixed. And following that logic, she was the ONLY one who could make the decision to move them somewhere else.

"Bradley," I said, "you're kind of a genius."

And I meant it. He was an amazing superhero trainer, but he was also half the brains of this operation, which made him more like a sidekick. A little like Bijou the Brave, actually.

And once again the computer lab was safe, thanks to @CAT and her quick-thinking sidekick, Bijou the Brave!

Just then, the garage door started to rumble again.

"Quick!" Bradley said. "They're already getting in their car!"

I put down my pencil and ran over, but I was a moment too late. The very-red-haired woman was already closing her door and her son was ducking into the passenger seat.

"Mind-control them!" Bradley urged. "Say something bad about Momo's house."

"Um…" I said, but I guess my mind was already racing with the new information about Principal Demerit and the Rats. I put my hands against my temples. "You hate that house," I started. "Because…your red hair would completely clash with the pink front door."

"Well," Bradley said as they drove away, "that *might* have done the trick."

I hoped he was right but—your hair clashes with the door? Even I knew it wasn't my finest work.

The Grand High Rat

Sure, they can be mangy and mean, but rats—like all living things—have an important role to play in nature. I learned on the Discovery Channel that they're scavengers: creatures that feed on garbage, dead plants, and animal carcasses. In a way, they're like nature's trash collectors—and Principal Demerit, the Grand High Rat, was no exception. Even though she wasn't eating rotting things out of the trash, she was constantly on the prowl for rotten behavior. Boots left in the middle of the hall where people might trip on them, kids wandering around when they were supposed to be in class, and apple cores thrown on the ground right beside the litter bin: all these things seemed to give her purpose in life.

I had to admit she was good at her job. Principal Demerit towered over the students, who trembled in her wake. She had beady eyes that didn't miss a thing, and every time I turned the corner, she seemed to be breezing by, barking out instructions— "Hats off!" "No gum!" "Put that pogo stick away!" Sometimes she didn't even need to speak. I once watched her break up an argument between two kids by tossing her super-shiny hair over one shoulder and giving them a single ice-cold look.

Each time I saw her, I'd put my hands to my temples to begin my mind control, but she was impossible to keep up with. Before I could get a thought in, she'd be gone—off to lecture the next kid who was using her outside voice inside or who had forgotten her gym shorts for the third time that week.

Principal Demerit didn't seem to care if she was bossing around R.R. Reginald kids or Gledhill kids. She'd obviously made herself right at home and would give a piece of her mind to anyone who disappointed her—something I discovered for myself after an unfortunate incident at track and field practice.

Even though the R.R. Reginald coach—Coach Donahue—was feeling better, the Rats showed up for our practice at second recess.

"Last week, both the Raccoons and the Gators had faster running times and better long jump distances than ever before," explained Coach Shipley when we'd all gathered around her and Coach Donahue in the field. "Coach Donahue and I have decided to continue training together so you can keep motivating each other."

"She thinks they're motivating us?" I huffed at Bradley. "More like torturing us!" I could still see the bruise on Bradley's leg from when Rick had tripped him on the track at our last practice.

"Let's warm up with two laps at a nice steady pace," Coach Shipley went on. "The finals are coming up this weekend, and we've got a lot of work to do!"

"Hear that, Clara?" Bossy Becky said, "accidentally" bumping into me as we made our way to the running oval. "Less than a week to go until I take the blue ribbon from you in the hundred-meter dash. Enjoy holding on to first place while you can."

"We'll see about that," I countered. "You'll have to catch me before you can beat me." Then I took off, my feet flying over the pavement like a set of turbo-powered triple-engine rockets.

INVENTION IDEA

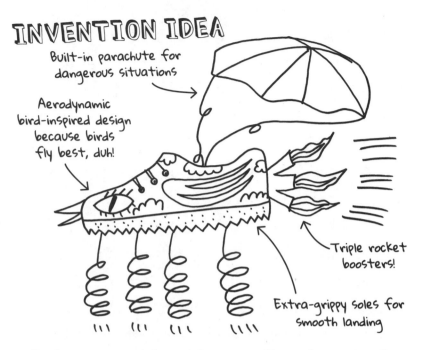

Built-in parachute for dangerous situations

Aerodynamic bird-inspired design because birds fly best, duh!

Triple rocket boosters!

Extra-grippy soles for smooth landing

"Like you could ever beat me!" Becky panted, catching up to me. "The only reason you won at the semis is because you soaked my shoes with hot-dog water."

"Just keep telling yourself that," I said over my shoulder as I started to sprint even faster.

A minute later, I heard Becky's stupid silver running shoes pounding against the pavement. She pulled up beside me, her ponytail swinging so wildly from side to side that it almost hit me in the face. I wanted to sprint ahead again, but I'd run so hard in the first lap that I was losing energy fast.

"You're going down, Clara Humble," Becky said, jogging next to me. "You *and* your dancing crocodile. If we win more blue ribbons than you at the track meet—*and we will*—we're going to send him for a swim in a port-a-potty this time!" She yelled this last part, then took off ahead of me.

I hardly remember it myself, but according to Bradley, what happened next was more than a little awe-inspiring. Anger shot through my veins like electricity, and without warning, I was flying. Well, not technically flying…but it felt that way, and Bradley said there was definitely a catlike quality to the way I went sailing through the air to pounce on my prey.

The next thing I knew, I was hanging on to Becky's back and we were tumbling over the pavement.

"Look out!"

"Runners down!"

The Rats and Gators who were right behind us didn't have enough time to stop or veer off course, and by the end of it, six different kids had joined the pileup—not that I noticed the exact count at the time. I was too busy pulling Becky's hair.

"Don't you *ever* threaten the Gator again! Do you hear me?" I said. But before Becky could respond, Coach Shipley and Coach Donahue were there, pulling us apart.

"Clara? What's gotten into you?" Coach Shipley asked.

"She started it!" I said, pointing to Becky, who was busy wailing over a tiny little scrape on her elbow.

But Coach Shipley didn't seem to care. She sent the other six kids, who had some scrapes and bruises, to the nurse's office, and Becky and me to the principal's office, where—as luck would have it—Principal Demerit was actually in for once, doing some paperwork. The situation wasn't great, but if I was ever going to get a chance to mind-control her, this was it!

"What's your name?" she asked, narrowing her eyes at me. She pushed her long hair over one shoulder, but it immediately slid back into place, nearly blinding me with its shine. "And why are you in my office?"

I gulped, then explained my side of the situation in as few words as I could.

"Is this true?" she asked Becky when I was done.

And that was when Becky turned on the waterworks. "I would *never* say a thing like that, Ms. Demerit!" she sobbed. "She just jumped on me! Out of nowhere! And now my elbow hurts SO much."

As she wailed and complained and threatened to sue me for bodily harm involving an elbow scrape, I quietly put my hands up against my temples and began to mind-control Principal Demerit.

LEAVE NOW!!!

TAKE ALL THE RATS WITH YOU!!!

NEVER COME BACK!!!

"Stop. I've heard quite enough," the principal said sternly, after she'd listened to Becky's sob story for several minutes. She turned to me and narrowed her eyes. "Clara, do you have a headache?"

"Umm…no. Not really," I said, dropping my hands from my head. I'd been concentrating as hard as I could, so I could only hope Principal Demerit and her Rats would be packing their books up and heading out before the end of the day.

"Threatening each other." She arched her eyebrows at Becky. "Pushing, shoving, hair pulling…" She glared at me. "I don't think I need to tell you that these things are *not* going to be tolerated over the few months we'll be sharing this building."

I felt my heart sink. The few *months*? How was it possible that my mind control had failed so spectacularly?

The bell rang, signaling the end of second recess, and Becky and I both stood up to go.

"Not so fast!" Principal Demerit said, pointing at our chairs. Becky and I both sat down. "I expect to see you cheering each other on at the track meet on the weekend. And in the meantime, I want you both in—"

She'd almost definitely been about to say the dreaded D-word (detention), but just then, a shout came from the hallway and Principal Demerit rose from her seat to see what was the matter.

"Give it back!" someone was yelling. The voice was familiar. *Very* familiar. I sprang to my feet and raced out into the hallway behind Principal Demerit. Halfway down the hall, which was quickly filling with students coming in from recess, I could see Bradley's little sister, Val. She was standing near the coat hooks for her class with her arms wrapped tightly around her waist. "Give it back right now," she said. Her voice quivered, as if she was about to cry.

A little boy was doing the pee-pee dance, and the teacher was rushing him into the kindergarten classroom. And meanwhile, most of the kids from Val's class were too busy fighting with their zippers or struggling out of their coats to notice what was going on.

Two big R.R. Reginald boys were tossing something in the air over Val's head. It took me a second to realize that it was Pumpkin—the stuffed toy that Val sleeps with and brings everywhere (even to school every day in her backpack).

"If you want it, come get it," the taller of the boys said, throwing it up even higher over Val's head to his snub-nosed friend, who rubbed it under his armpit and then tossed it back.

Bradley came in the doors from outside just then. He was still wearing his gym clothes and looked sweaty from track practice.

"Hey!" he shouted when he spotted the boys tormenting his sister. His face went bright red and his fists clenched. I don't think I'd ever seen him so angry before. "That's my sister's pumpkin. Give it back."

None of them had noticed Principal Demerit yet—although they would soon. She was storming down the hallway like a hurricane.

"Go long," the taller Rat shouted to his friend. With his eyes on the incoming pumpkin, the boy ran backward down the hall, narrowly missed colliding with three different kids, and then bumped right into Principal Demerit.

"What's this about?" she asked, with fire in

her eyes, right before the pumpkin came sailing through the air and hit her in the head.

The Grand High Rat gave a small, sharp intake of breath and then she started yelling...loudly. The sound filled the hallway and bounced off the walls. Most of the kids froze on the spot, and some of the teachers rushed out to see what was wrong. Everyone was so frightened, in fact, that nobody else seemed to notice what I noticed...

Ever so casually, as she was busy ordering her Rats to apologize to Val and go directly to the office, Principal Demerit put one hand on top of her head and pushed at her hair. Her entire scalp seemed to shift slightly to the right, then she pushed it back in place and straightened the ends of her hair.

Principal Demerit was wearing a wig!

That explained everything. For starters—how her hair was *that* shiny. But also why my brain waves weren't able to penetrate her skull.

Then it occurred to me: it also explained why I hadn't been able to mind-control Momo when she'd been wearing a kerchief for cleaning—and why my backyard practice with Bradley had failed that time. It was a chilly night and he'd had his hat on.

Suddenly, it all became clear! If I was going to mind-control the Grand High Rat and get rid of her and her Rat minions once and for all, I was going to have to get that wig off first.

But how?

10

Plan A:
Operation Chinchilla

When the bus pulled up at our stop that afternoon, my dad was standing on the corner in the rain. The instant I saw him, I suspected that something was very wrong, and I knew it for sure when he said this:

"Hey, sweetie. Good day? I thought we could go grab some ice cream."

What was it with adults, ice cream, and terrible news lately?

He didn't even wait until we got to Baskin-Robbins to drop it on me, and when he did, he did it in the most infuriating way possible.

"I've got some *good* news." He plastered on a smile as we rounded the corner, huddling underneath his big black umbrella. "It looks like there's going to be a new kid in the neighborhood. A family has put in an offer on Momo's house!"

I stopped right in the middle of a puddle.

"It's actually a boy about your age and his mom. They're having an inspector look at the place soon, and if everything seems in order, they should be moving in next month."

When my dad saw the look on my face, he dropped the fake grin and reached out to touch my shoulder.

"Clara, I know this isn't easy. Momo wanted to be the one to tell you herself, but she's out of town until tomorrow. She's staying at her sister's place with the cats until the home inspection is over. You'll see, sweetie. Eventually, you'll get used to having a new neighbor. We all will. Do you want to talk about it?"

But I didn't want to talk about it. And I was *never*

going to get used to it. I just turned around and started for home, not even caring that I'd left my dad behind with the umbrella and I was getting drenched to the bone. Actually, it was better that way. At least with the rain streaming down my face, nobody could see how hard I was crying.

In the life of every superhero, there comes a dark day…one where the obstacles seem too insurmountable and the villains too villainous.

I had failed, and my failings were great. Momo would be moving far away to a place filled with old people where she might (literally) get bored to death, and all my efforts to rid the school of Rats had so far been futile. Even now that I knew the key to getting them to leave lay in mind-controlling Principal Demerit, I couldn't do it because of her impenetrable super-shiny wig!

And now, Becky had threatened the Gledhill Gator! If they won more blue ribbons than us, she was going to push him into a port-a-potty at Sunday's track meet—and if she pushed him into a port-a-potty, our team spirit might just go with him.

I moped around all night and barely nibbled at my tuna casserole while my parents exchanged worried glances across the dinner table. And even though Bradley did his best to rally my spirits when we met in his backyard for some hole digging, it was no use.

The rest of the week at school I didn't even bother flicking the cafeteria lights on and off with the powers of my mind, and on Friday morning, I passed up a perfectly good opportunity to spill a sand bucket full of dirty puddle water on Bossy Becky's head, despite the fact that somebody had left it on the playground equipment and she was standing right underneath it.

But if there's one thing that's certain in this world of ours, it's that after the sun sets, it rises again. And when things seem most hopeless, a hero will emerge, or re-emerge, or at least get out of bed at (surprise!) exactly 7:14 the next morning and trip over a big popcorn bowl that she (in her despair) accidentally left on her bedroom floor the night before and then bump into her bookcase only to have *this* flutter out from between the pages of an old sketchbook:

I picked up my drawing, letting its message sink in while my toe throbbed. @Cat would never give up, and neither could I!

I still had time to protect my school from the tyranny of the Rats. I just had to think of an ingenious plan. And sure, things looked bad for Momo's move…but the new family hadn't moved in just yet, had they?

That morning, as I was mulling things over and eating a bowl of Cheerios while watching cartoons, I found out that fate had stepped in to give me a helping hand.

"So what did they say was wrong with it?" I overheard my mom ask my dad as she sat down across the kitchen table from him.

"A soft spot in the roof," he said. "Momo hasn't seen any leaks, but the home inspector is saying it could be rotting out. The buyer wants her to replace the whole thing."

I kicked my supersonic hearing into high gear so I'd be certain not to miss a word.

"When it's not even leaking? That's crazy! Why doesn't the buyer just offer a lower price and fix it herself?"

My dad made a mumbling noise in response.

"She should just turn down the offer, then," my mom said decisively.

"I think she might," my dad answered.

"Yessssss!" I said under my breath.

"She says she'll probably go ahead with another open house tomorrow and see what happens," he went on.

I felt my spirits sink again, but only a little. Even though Momo still wanted to sell her house, this turn of events bought me time to figure something out. Plus I could still find a way to get rid of the Rats before they made good on their threat of pushing the Gator into a port-a-potty—*if* I thought fast. But I knew I couldn't do it alone!

"Mm-ah goin' to Bwadley's," I shouted in the direction of the kitchen. My mouth was full of Cheerios, but I had no time to waste chewing and swallowing. I half-stuffed my feet into a pair of sneakers and ran out the door, across my yard and into Bradley's, skidding straight into our newest giant hole and sending up a cloud of dust.

"Good news!" I announced, wiping a soggy (and now dirty) Cheerio off my cheek. Then I told Bradley how the sale of Momo's house had fallen through. "I still have time to think of a plan," I said. "But I also need your help finding a way to get that wig off Principal Demerit, *and* we can't let the Rats get away with pushing the Gator into a port-a-potty."

"Don't worry," Bradley said. "I've already got the wig covered. All we have to do is use your powers of hydrokinesis to spill something on Principal Demerit's head. Then she'll have to take her wig off to let it dry. Meanwhile, you mind-control her and—*poof*—the Rats leave."

"Hmmmmm…" I said thoughtfully. It wasn't a *bad* plan. But it left a lot up to chance. What if Principal Demerit just used a towel to dry off her wig instead of taking it off? Also, if she really *did* need to take it off, she'd probably go into her office and close the door before removing it. And even if we *could* find a way to get her to take her wig off somewhere public, like the hallway or the gym, she'd probably just put it right back on again after shaking the water off it. And that might not give me enough time to mind-control her. I mean, my powers had definitely gotten stronger…but I wasn't sure I could work under that kind of pressure yet!

No, if we were going to do this, we had to make sure we did it right. We'd need to get that wig off and keep it off for at least a few minutes, and we'd need to do it in a place where Principal Demerit would have nowhere to hide.

"The track meet," I said. "It's tomorrow! It's out in the open. It's the only place that's *guaranteed* to work."

"Maybe…" Bradley said doubtfully. "But what about the Rats pushing the Gator into the port-a-potty if they win the most ribbons? How are we going to get the wig off *and* stop that?"

I still wasn't sure, but I knew there had to be a way. We turned to a fresh page in Bradley's

archeology log book and spent the rest of the
morning brainstorming and scheming, plotting
and planning. But it wasn't until after lunch that
we finally came up with it—the Rat Trap.

"It's genius!" I said, looking at the sketch we'd
made, which was covered all over with arrows and
instructions.

"It's practically foolproof," Bradley concurred.

"It's inspired," I added, because it really was
pretty great.

"But we're going to need a few things," Bradley
pointed out. "And we're going to need them fast."

"Don't worry," I said. "I'm on it."

And for the first
time all week, I had
a huge grin on my
face.

I spent the rest of the afternoon collecting Rat Trap supplies. Having them ready to go gave me an amazing sense of calm…but by the time we'd finished dinner, I still didn't have a plan for Momo, and I was running out of time. Real estate agent Susan Swan (and her big hair) had already stopped by to put the Open House sign up, and as I looked at it out the window, I felt like crying again.

What could I possibly do? Momo had left for her sister's place again, taking Fatty-Fatty-Two-Tip and Wiggles with her, and I knew I didn't stand a chance of mind-controlling every person who went in to see the house. For one thing, the open house was going to last all day. I'd be at the track meet until noon, and even after that, I'd definitely need to eat and go to the bathroom at some point. Also, it was getting colder with every passing day. A lot of people were probably going to be wearing hats.

I had just shut the curtains and slumped down on my bed when Bijou hopped up onto the platform in her cage and started to scratch her paws against the bars. "Not now, doodlebug," I said. "I'm trying to think of a plan."

She scratched even harder, then started hopping around on her jungle gym.

"Bijou!" I scolded. "PLEASE be quiet. I need to think of a way to keep Momo from moving. The last thing I need right now is a chinchilla—" I stopped mid-sentence. Suddenly, it all connected in my brain.

Buyers don't like the smell of animals.

FOR SALE

Good news! Momo's open house will still go ahead!

SUPER CLARA'S hidden power: Communicate with chinchillas!

Maybe a chinchilla was EXACTLY what I needed! "Oh, snookie-wookums!" I walked over and lifted her out of her cage. "You're brilliant! This might actually work."

I decided to wait until nightfall so that I could work under the cover of darkness. Then I put Operation Chinchilla into effect. As I tiptoed down the stairs, I could see my parents in the living room. They were snuggled up on the sofa watching a TV show about how wristwatches are made.

"Shhh!" I whispered to Bijou, who was tucked tightly against my chest between my sweatshirt and T-shirt. As quietly as mice (or other larger rodents), we ducked past the doorway of the living room and into the kitchen. From there, it was just a few steps to the door that led to the garage. I inched it open, willing it not to squeak. And then, just like I'd planned—

Sensing that I was within ten feet of it, the garage door rattled to life, opening wide to let Bijou and me out.

My parents must have heard it, but not surprisingly, they didn't bother getting up off the couch. The door had been opening and closing for a few weeks now. Even the neighbors who'd complained at first were ignoring it.

I dashed down the driveway and along the path to Momo's back door. As always, it was unlocked. I pushed it open and stepped into her darkened kitchen.

Without Momo or the cats, everything seemed too still—not to mention too clean. Momo's clunky green gardening shoes were missing from their usual spot near the radiator, and without all the artwork I'd given her over the years, the fridge looked naked.

I tiptoed into the dining room. Momo must have spent ages scrubbing it, because there was no sign of the paint I'd made Fatty-Fatty tip over.

There were other weird things, too…the curtains were open and the sofas had been moved around. It already didn't look much like Momo's house.

"Oh, Bijou," I said, giving my chinchilla one last hug before setting her down on the floor. "I hope we're not too late. You know what to do tomorrow, right?"

She looked up at me, twitched her nose twice to tell me I had nothing to worry about, and then went off to sniff one of the houseplants.

"Well…I guess my work here is done," I said softly. I walked back out into the darkness, shutting the door behind me.

Plan B:
The Rat Trap

As it turns out, the best-laid plans (especially when those plans involve setting chinchillas free in other people's houses) often fail. And not only do they fail, but sometimes they are total and complete disasters—with destruction on a massive scale. But I'm getting ahead of myself. The part I should start with is the track and field finals, where the Rat Trap went off without a hitch… kind of.

It was a lucky (but hardly surprising) thing that I woke up at 7:14 that morning, because I still had a lot to get done before we left for the finals at Blinkstone Park.

For one thing, I had to find my lucky underpants—the ones with the shooting stars on them. (I did a timed trial once and they actually *do* make me run faster.) Then I had to pack my things:

- Running shoes
- Water bottle
- Hot pink Band-Aids in case of blisters
- Stopwatch
- Extra-value pack of twenty fly-fishing hooks
- Fifty feet of see-through string
- Sidewalk chalk in rainbow colors
- MP3 player loaded with the "Chicken Dance" song

When I was done that, I had to start bugging my parents to hurry up. They're big fans of sleeping in on Sunday mornings, and even when they *do* get up, they'll sip cold coffee and read sections of the newspaper aloud for *hours* if I don't stop them.

"Let's go let's go let's *goooooo!*" I sang. I was standing at the door with my shoes and windbreaker already on.

"All right, Clara. Hold your horses," my mom said. She went into the kitchen and poured her coffee into a travel mug. "We'll get there in plenty of time."

Bradley was already waiting for us on his front steps when our car rounded the corner. "Do you have everything?" he whispered as he got in.

I winked twice, which was our secret sign for "A-OK."

"Have you had breakfast yet, Bradley?" my mom said, turning around in the front seat. "I brought some spelt chocolate chip muffins."

I looked at Bradley and tugged furiously on my earlobe—the signal for "No-go." The last thing he needed before track finals was a spelt muffin sitting like a small boulder in his stomach.

"No, thank you, Mrs. Humble," he answered, picking up on my covert communication. "I just had cornflakes."

When we got to the field, my parents immediately parked themselves on the bleachers and opened up the newspapers they'd brought along, which gave us a chance to get to work. We'd just finished our preparations when the first group of kids arrived—led by none other than Bossy Becky of the R.R. Reginald Rats. Just like we'd predicted, she took the bait straight away.

"You guys!" she called out to Darla and Joanna, who were close behind her, as always. "Look what somebody drew over here!"

"Obviously, this is our area!" She laughed, then set her stuff down inside the circle we'd drawn on the ground in sidewalk chalk.

Seeing this, Bradley, who was crouched by the flagpole tying his shoe, gave me two big winks. I double-winked back.

Before long, the stands started to fill with parents and the field started to fill with kids from Gledhill, R.R. Reginald, A.Y. Jackson, and all the other schools in town. The teams were grouped together in different spots on the lawn, talking, laughing, and bouncing around, partly from nerves and partly from trying to keep warm in the chilly morning air. The mascots were also out in full force with the Gledhill Gator (obviously) leading the pack in terms of style and attitude.

GOOO OO GATORS!

Gattitude to spare

Of course, the other mascots weren't exactly trying. The R.R. Reginald Raccoon already had a mustache from drinking so much "free juice" from the vat of orange energy drink. Meanwhile, the A.Y. Jackson Blue Jay was fluttering around aimlessly and the Oakley Octopus had only four of her arms on.

"Moms and dads, boys and girls!" one of the refs announced over the microphone. "I'd like to welcome you to the Annual Gleason City Track and Field Finals!"

There was a polite round of applause from the parents, some hooting and hollering from the kids, and an ear-splitting "WHOOP!" from the Gator.

"Before we start our first event—which will be the hundred-meter dash..." (When the ref named our event, Becky glared over at me from the Winner's Circle. I glared right back.) "...I'd like to go over a few announcements and ground rules for the morning. First and most importantly, you'll find the port-a-potties and hand-wash stations directly behind us on the northeast side of the field."

That was when I noticed that Bradley, who had stationed himself behind the row of principals and other official adults near the front, was waving to get my attention. He winked twice, giving me the go-ahead.

It was now or never. I wiggled past Roger and Will so that I was standing closer to the front of our group, then I put my hands against my temples, and using all the powers of my mind, I focused on a spot on the ground just behind the principals.

For a second, I was sure I saw something move. I gave Bradley a questioning look, but he tugged on his ear. A no-go. I stepped around Siu to get closer, and I tried again, focusing even harder this time.

"Students are to wear their team shirts and race numbers at all times," the ref continued, "and there will be no rough-housing or name-calling."

I tilted my head to one side and stared as hard as I could. Still nothing. Then I realized what was wrong: I wasn't mad about anything! I needed to get angry. Really angry! And fast. But how? Thankfully, Bossy Becky and her friends helped me out.

"I would also like to remind students that the duck pond, although shallow, can still be a dangerous body of water," the ref went on. "It's also a natural habitat for ducks, frogs, and other animals and should not be disturbed."

"He forgot to say it's the natural habitat of Gators who can barely dance," I overheard Darla say to Becky and Joanna under her breath.

"Actually," said Becky, "the pond's too good for the Gator. It belongs at the bottom of one of those." She pointed to the row of port-a-potties, and they all snickered. "And that's exactly where it'll be when we win all the blue ribbons."

I wanted to march right over and tell her to say

that again to my face, if she dared, but of course, I didn't. Instead (much like @Cat did that time the human foolishly tried to give her a bath), I harnessed my incredible rage, then directed it to serve my purposes.

There was a small flash of metal in the sunlight, and not a moment too soon!

"And now, I'd like to invite Abby McDonald from R.R. Reginald Public School to lead us in singing the national anthcm."

A tiny mouselike girl stepped forward and took the microphone. Even from where I was standing,

I could see that her hands were shaking—but it turned out she had nothing to be nervous about. The second she opened her mouth, a hush fell over the field. Her singing voice was so unexpectedly big, not to mention beautiful.

Part of me would have liked to listen to her all day, but I didn't have that luxury. One of the flag bearers was getting ready to hoist the flag. The time for action was at hand.

First, I focused my electrokinetic powers on the microphone. Almost immediately, it crackled, then shorted out, leaving Mouse-Girl looking baffled—especially because, a second later, the sound of

her beautiful clear voice was replaced by the irritating-but-oh-so-danceable opening bars of the "Chicken Dance." Total confusion, and a little bit of chicken dancing, broke out. The refs were running back and forth, looking for the source of the music. Some of the parents were trying to get their kids to stop dancing, while others were making a completely embarrassing attempt to join in. In fact, things were so out of control that it took almost a minute before everyone else noticed the other thing that was happening.

MY WIG!

The fishing hooks that I'd levitated with my powers had snagged in Principal Demerit's wig, just as we'd hoped they would. Meanwhile, the clear plastic fishing lines that were attached to the hooks held tight to the flag, where Bradley had secretly sewn them before the meet began.

So when the national anthem had started and the flag was hoisted—the wig went with it. It looked like a big, black, shiny-winged bird, flapping its way up, up into the sky.

Principal Demerit looked back and forth and then finally up, as she realized what had happened. She jumped once, then twice, trying to grab her wig, but it was already out of reach, so instead she tried to cover her head with one hand—not that it did any good. All around the field, kids had started pointing and whispering. And there were more than a few giggles.

I'm not sure what I'd been expecting Principal Demerit's hair to look like underneath her wig, but I definitely hadn't guessed it would be styled in short, bright purple spikes. It looked like a purple puffer fish was trying to eat her head. It was so cool that I couldn't take my eyes off it... and for a second, I stared like everyone else, but then I snapped myself out of it. Some of the adults were already gathering around, trying to help retrieve the wig. Luckily, the fishing line had snagged in the flagpole rope and they were having trouble lowering it. Still, I had some serious mind-controlling to do and no time to waste!

I focused like I'd never focused before! I was concentrating so hard, in fact, that I had no idea how much time had passed. Had it been a full two minutes (the amount of time Bradley and I had figured I'd need)? I had no idea.

TAKE YOUR WIG AND RATS...

GO NOW...

LEAVE GLEDHILL...

DO NOT RETURN...

Luckily, Bradley, who had my new stopwatch, had been timing everything down to the second. He winked twice for A-OK and I breathed a small sigh of relief. Then he motioned with his head toward the vat of super-sugary orange drink.

Right! It was time for my last great heroic act. I put my hands back up to my temples and thought about Bossy Becky and her Rats invading our school...about Momo moving far, far away to watch a boring fish tank with a bunch of old people...about my parents keeping secrets from me...and about teachers and principals always telling kids what to do without ever once asking what *we* wanted. I thought about everything in the world that made me maddest of all—every wrong, every injustice!

But nothing happened.

I looked to Bradley and frantically tugged on my ear.

"Try again!" he mouthed, and I did, but it was no good. Maybe the vat of orange sugary drink was just too heavy, or maybe my powers were depleted by all the amazing feats I'd just performed. Whatever the reason, I didn't see any choice. I was going to have to take matters into my own (actual) hands.

I sprinted with a speed that would have served me well in the hundred-meter dash and ducked behind the bushes on the other side of the track. Then, using all my might, I heaved the orange-drink vat until it tipped, landing with a thud on the ground, where it glug-glugged a sea of neon sugar water right into the Winner's Circle, where the Rats were all gathered.

"What the heck?!" Becky shrieked.

"Move, you guys! Move!" Darla yelled at some R.R. Reginald kids who were still busy chicken dancing and hadn't noticed what was happening to their shoes.

"Ugh!" Joanna said, stamping her feet against the clean pavement outside the circle. "My sneakers are all sticky!"

"It's like there's glue on them," one of the Rats said.

"How am I supposed to do the running long jump now?" whined another.

"Smells good, though," added the R.R. Reginald Raccoon, unhelpfully. "Orangey."

And with that, I sank down onto the ground behind the bushes, exhausted from all my efforts but confident that I'd done my very best to set things right again.

"Wait a second!" I heard a familiar bossy voice say. "Is that Clara? Clara Humble? Behind the bushes?"

My eyes flicked open and I immediately made myself into a tiny ball, hoping I might suddenly develop the power of invisibility, or at least blend into the foliage—but no such luck.

"Clara Humble is hiding behind the bushes. She spilled the energy drink! On purpose! So we won't be able to compete!" Becky announced. "You guys, go tell the coach and the referees that she wet our shoes *again*," she instructed Joanna and Darla, then she leaned over the bush so her face loomed above me. "Clara Humble, you are so dead," she said with a satisfied smirk.

And it was true. I sort of was…but the worst part hadn't even happened yet.

"Is this true, Clara?" Coach Shipley asked when she came to find me. She was followed by one of the referees and by Principal Demerit (whose wig was now covering her spikes, although her face was so red I worried her head might explode and send it flying off again).

"Maybe?" I said, which, looking back on it, probably wasn't the best answer.

"Ummm…Principal Demerit?" It was a tiny voice, coming from a tiny person. Mouse-Girl was pulling the sleeves of her windbreaker down over her hands, looking flustered.

"Not now, Abby," Principal Demerit said, focusing her eyes on me like lasers.

"But," the mouse went on, "I just thought you might want to know…I saw who put the hooks in your hair and broke the microphone, too."

I did a double take. Getting caught for tipping the juice vat was one thing, but how could anyone possibly suspect me of anything else? I'd been with my teammates the whole time! Unless Mouse-Girl could somehow sense my powers?

"I saw everything. It was him," she said, pointing at Bradley, who was standing just outside the puddle of orange drink, staring at his feet.

Powerless

Want to know the real difference between superheroes and regular people? It's simple. Superheroes *always* know right from wrong. Regular people get it all mixed up. (Well, that and we don't usually wear capes.)

Is it so wrong to want your school to be free of Rats with bad attitudes or to take revenge for the injustice done to a dancing alligator? Is it some kind of crime to want your best friend on earth close by—preferably right next door? Or selfish to wish she could always be happy, playing Snap and Rummy with you instead of Solitaire alone?

If you ask me, the answer to all those questions is no. And yet, for some reason, it *is* wrong to deeply embarrass a principal, interrupt the national anthem with the "Chicken Dance," singlehandedly ruin a track meet, and release a medium-sized rodent into someone's house to make those wishes come true. Very wrong. Very, very wrong.

I realized this the moment Principal Franco, Principal Demerit, and my parents started asking Bradley and me why on earth we'd done such a thing…and it became more than clear when we pulled into our driveway, setting the garage door off and alerting Momo of our return.

She came storming down her pathway to stand on our front lawn with her hands on her hips.

"Maureen?" my mom said, getting out of the passenger seat. "I thought you were at your sister's place until the open house was over."

"Oh, I was. But it looks like there isn't going to be an open house today." She narrowed her eyes at me. "Well? Is there something you want to say for yourself, Clara?"

Although I had a pretty good idea, I still didn't know *exactly* what Momo was mad about, so I decided not to comment.

"Clara?" my mom asked.

"How did Bijou get into my house?" Momo prompted. "And *don't* tell me she just wandered over."

"What?!" my dad said.

"Do you have any idea the damage you've done?" Momo asked me. "Or how dangerous that was for Bijou? She could get very sick! Not to mention that someone could have stepped on her or let her escape into the yard."

My eyes ping-ponged back and forth, trying to keep up with everything Momo was saying and my parents' growing disappointment in me. What damage? Why would Bijou be sick? Had she accomplished her mission? Judging by how mad Momo was and the fact that the open house had been canceled, I was pretty sure she had.

"You let Bijou loose in Momo's house!? *What* is going on with you, Clara?" my dad added. It looked like Momo and my parents were ready to stand there all day, staring me down. I figured I'd better say *something*.

"The real estate agent told you on the phone that buyers think animals smell bad," I said, turning to Momo. "I figured…if Bijou was there, and she stank up the place a little, maybe nobody would want your house. And then maybe you could stay."

Momo put a hand over her mouth and breathed out heavily through her nose.

"Could someone tell me what happened?" I asked softly. "Why could Bijou get sick?"

Momo suddenly looked very, very tired.

"Come," she said. "I want you to see what you've done with your own eyes."

Momo led the way up her front path, pushed open her front door, and motioned for me to step inside.

The first thing I noticed was that the curtains in Momo's living room were tilted sideways, falling off the rod. Then, as my eyes adjusted to the light, I saw something else: tiny bits of tissue—almost like Kleenex that has been through the wash—were scattered like a dusting of snow over the floor. At first I thought maybe it was stuffing from a sofa that had exploded, but then my eyes drifted toward the lower part of the walls, which were usually covered in pink-and-blue-striped wallpaper. At roughly chinchilla height, the walls were bare in some patches, while shreds of wallpaper hung off them in others. It almost looked like a gang of very short teenagers had thrown a wild party. Either that, or some kind of crime scene.

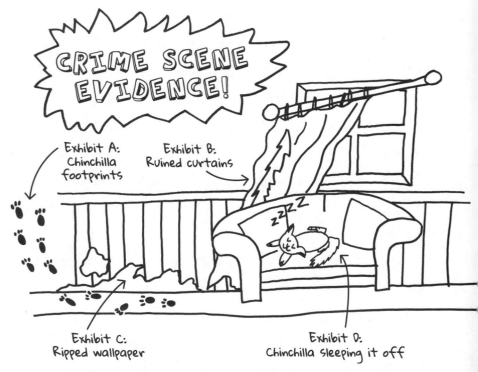

CRIME SCENE EVIDENCE!

Exhibit A: Chinchilla footprints

Exhibit B: Ruined curtains

Exhibit C: Ripped wallpaper

Exhibit D: Chinchilla sleeping it off

"Bijou did this?" I said, still not quite believing it. I knew she was a good chewer (she'd once eaten the

shoelaces off my gym shoes over Christmas break),
but this was extremely advanced work, even for her.

"When the agent got here to start the open house,
she thought there'd been a break-in," Momo said.
"Then she found Bijou asleep on the sofa. Susan
thought she was a large rat. She almost hit her
with a shoe. It's just lucky for you that the first
people to come to the open house were the mother
and son who made an offer last week. The little boy
used to have a chinchilla in his classroom and told
Susan it must be a pet. Even still, we can only hope
Bijou doesn't get sick from all the wallpaper paste
she ate.

"It's also lucky for you—and for me," Momo went
on, "that the mother and son have changed their
minds about the roof. They've decided to buy the
house as is…and they were planning to take down
the wallpaper anyway."

"Clara, I think you owe Momo the biggest
apology of your life," my mom cut in, using her
most serious voice.

But Momo held up her hands to stop me. "I don't
think I want to hear it," she said. "Not right now. I
think you should probably leave."

My dad put his hands on my shoulders and guided me out of Momo's house—which wasn't Momo's house anymore, not really. I don't remember walking into my own house or up the stairs. I barely remember placing Bijou, who was fast asleep in my arms, back in her cage. All I remember is feeling like the place where my heart used to be was now an empty, aching hole.

DISCLAIMER
The actions and opinions of SUPER CLARA in no way reflect those held by @CAT or @CAT Corporation

That night—like I so often do—I spilled my milk at dinner.

"Oh, Clara!" my mom said—like she always does. "Try to be more careful!"

She sounded even more annoyed than usual, and I guess I couldn't blame her. I really *had* been the worst daughter ever that day, not to mention the worst friend and superhero.

"Is it okay if I go to Bradley's?" I asked after I'd cleared my plate. I expected my parents to say no. They had every right to ground me for life. But maybe they were just sick of looking at me and realizing what a colossal disappointment I was.

"Home by dark," my mom said, "and come right back if Bradley's mother says he can't play."

I walked to the back of the yard. "Bradley? You here?" I called out flatly as I wiggled between the gap in our fences. And surprisingly, he was. At first I thought maybe his mother couldn't stand to look at him, either, but then I noticed the trash bag in his hand.

"Hey," he said, smiling at me awkwardly.

"Hey," I answered, kicking some dirt back into our latest giant hole.

For a long moment, we didn't know what to say to each other.

"I'm supposed to just take the garbage out and then come right back in. My mom's pretty mad," he said finally.

"My mom and dad are, too," I said.

I didn't want him to get caught talking to me

and get into even more trouble, but I knew I had to ask. Otherwise, wondering until morning was going to drive me crazy.

"Why did you move the fish hooks and unplug the microphone instead of letting me use my powers?" I asked.

He shrugged. "I wanted to help you. I could tell you probably weren't going to be able to do it."

"Did you, um, ever help me with anything else?" I asked, giving him my most serious look.

"Maybe a few things," he mumbled, shuffling his feet. "Like sometimes I flicked the cafeteria lights on and off for you when I was on my way to the bathroom…and then that time when the bucket of water spilled at Momo's house…and maybe a few other things. And I guess I started it all when I was mad at Becky for pushing the Gator into the pond. I kind of nudged your hot-dog water."

I know it sounds dramatic, but I sank down on my knees as the weight of reality hit me. "So I don't really have any super powers, then," I said. I felt so completely stupid. I mean, *of course* I didn't have any super powers!

THINGS THAT ARE POWERLESS

| Dad's phone after he dropped it in his coffee! | Our house last year after Dad plugged in a "major new invention" | SUPER CLARA |

"That's not true!" Bradley said. "Or at least, I doubt it is. What about the raisin you moved with your mind? Or the Christmas tree tinsel that floated across the room that time we were at your house? Or how you made the Rats hate our school? And even my mom has noticed that thing about lightbulbs and batteries dying when you're nearby. Practically every time you come over, she has to put fresh batteries in the Wii controllers. And why do you *always* wake up at 7:14? That's pretty strange."

It was nice of Bradley to try to cheer me up, but the raisin could have been moved by something hitting the picnic table. And the Christmas tree tinsel could have been the wind from my dad opening the front door. The Rats hated our school

191

because they hated everything. And sometimes we played Wii for hours, so of course the batteries died. And what was the big deal about waking up at 7:14, anyway? It was *totally* useless!

"Plus realsuperpowers.org said it was all about confidence. I thought that if you believed you could do it, then maybe you really could..." He trailed off, looking guilty.

"Hey," Bradley said all of a sudden. He sank down to the ground beside me. At first I thought he was going to give me a hug or something, but then he reached into the hole. "What's that? See there? It looks like the edge of some old paper, wrapped in plastic. Wait here. I'll get a shovel. It could be a treasure map."

If anything, it looked more like a moldy old newspaper in a clear plastic bag—the kind the newspaper delivery guy uses whenever it rains— but I didn't tell Bradley that. I figured he'd discover it for himself in a minute, anyway.

He came back with a spade, then jumped into the hole and started to dig furiously, glancing up at his house every so often to make sure his mom wasn't watching out the window.

"I think I've almost got it now," he said.

Even though it went against everything the archeology book taught, Bradley set his shovel down and pulled hard. The plastic bag came out of the dirt, sending him flying backward.

"Here." He stood up and handed me the bag. "Open it. I'm too nervous to do it myself."

So I did...

"Holy cheese!" Bradley said, leaning in close to see the map I'd just unfolded. It was from a carnival they held every year in the Save-o-Rama parking lot downtown.

I brushed a bit of stray dirt off the map and smoothed the creases against my knees. It looked like a piece of garbage, really. And there was probably a perfectly reasonable explanation for how it had gotten into Bradley's backyard. Maybe one time—a long time ago, before Bradley and Val moved in—some other kids lived here. Maybe they went to the fair and then buried the map in the backyard for fun. Or maybe it blew by on garbage day and fell into a hole someone was digging.

But then, why the plastic bag? Didn't that make it seem like someone was trying to protect it? Like maybe—just maybe—someone had put it there on purpose? Because it led to something valuable? It wasn't *that* crazy of an idea.

And that was when I understood why Bradley had tipped over the bucket at Momo's house, shut off the cafeteria lights, and lied to me about the hot-dog water.

My super powers weren't real—I knew that now—but Bradley had wanted to believe in them for the exact same reason I kept hoping that rusty barbecue flippers, old mint tins, and moldy fairground maps *might* be pirate treasure…because it made Bradley happy. And also because you never knew…

"I'm not *really* mad at you, by the way," I said.

"I know you were just trying to help. Sorry you got in so much trouble."

"That's okay," he said. "So did you. I was scared for a second there that Principal Demerit was going to strangle us both."

"Yeah, if Bossy Becky didn't do it first."

Neither of us knew quite what to say after that, so to break the awkwardness, I stared hard at the map.

"Hey," I said all of a sudden. "Look at that."

Bradley squinted at the spot I was pointing to on the yellowed page. A less experienced treasure hunter might have mistaken it for a coffee ring, but there it was, clear as day—a circle. And inside it, written in faint pencil, was an *X*, directly above the spot where the Twirling Teacup ride always was.

"*X* marks the spot," I said.

Bradley's entire face lit up, and despite what a horrible day it had been, I found myself smiling, too.

The world was an amazing place, after all. And olden-days pirates *had* existed. So who was I to say that a trunk of gold coins *wasn't* buried in the parking lot at the Save-o-Rama? Honestly, I really hoped it was.

The Momo-mobile

Except for our excitement over the treasure map and the plans Bradley and I started making for a dig in the spring, the coming week promised to be *very* un-super.

For one thing, I had to face Becky and the rest of the Rats, who had decided I was now their sworn enemy. Plus my parents and Bradley's mom had both agreed that we needed to apologize to Principal Demerit right away...a terrifying idea!

It's no exaggeration to say that when Bradley and I knocked on her office door on Monday, I was feeling about an eighth of an inch tall.

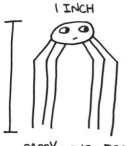
1 INCH
DADDY LONG LEGS

1/2 INCH
BUMBLEBEE

1/4 INCH
ANT

1/8 INCH
CLARA HUMBLE

"Yes?" she snapped when she saw us standing at the door.

All we could see were the tops of her eyes peering at us above her computer screen, but that was scary enough.

Thankfully, Bradley was feeling braver than I was. "We came to say sorry," he said. "For your wig. We feel really bad."

That much was true. Even though her secret spiky purple hair was amazing, and I couldn't understand why she didn't want everyone to see it all the time, pulling off her wig and embarrassing her in front of a whole crowd of people had been a really mean thing to do. I wished we'd never thought of it.

"Come in," she said in a surprisingly soft tone.

Bradley and I exchanged worried looks. Was this her way of luring us into her office so she could feed us poisoned candy, force us to stand with our noses pressed against the wall, or build a cage out of yardsticks and lock us inside it for the rest of the day? There was no way of knowing for sure, but we couldn't *not* do what she said. We took a few steps toward her desk. My knees were shaking.

She rolled her chair over to see around her computer and fixed us with a steady stare. "All night I wondered: Why did you do that?"

Bradley looked like he was about to throw up, so I knew it was my turn to take the lead.

"I guess…" I said, stopping to find the right words. "We were hoping we could make you want to leave Gledhill. We kind of want our school back. Still, though, we're very sorry," I added.

"Ah," she said simply, like that was all she needed to know, then she grabbed a pen and started writing something down on a piece of paper. From where we were standing, I couldn't read it, but my mind raced with the possibilities. Was she figuring out how many months (or years?) of detention we each deserved? Or writing a note to our parents to explain why we were being permanently expelled from the fourth grade? Or jotting down a reminder to make us scrub toilets for the rest of the year? Or maybe recording the details of our crime so she could pass us over to the police, who would lock us up in children's prison, where we'd rot away with some *real* rats?

"Tell me," Principal Demerit said, after a minute.

"What do you think I want?"

"Ummmm," I said. I honestly didn't know. Rows of completely quiet students saluting her in perfectly clean hallways? An even shinier wig? World domination? She seemed evil enough that almost anything was possible.

"Do you think I want to be here?" She didn't wait for an answer. "No," she said. "I want my own school back, too. And do you think my students want to be here?"

This time we knew the answer.

"No," we both said.

"And yet, here we are, together in a bad situation, and we need to make the best of it." She put her note aside, then picked up a stack of papers and dropped them with a thud on her desk. Bradley and I both jumped at the sound.

"Maybe," she went on, with a cold look in her beady eyes, "we can even make a few new friends while we're at it?"

We nodded like bobbleheads.

"But most of all," she continued, not blinking even once, "no matter what, we treat each other kindly. Understood?"

We nodded again.

"And for the next two weeks, every day at lunch hour, I'll be seeing you here for detention."

We nodded one more time.

Two weeks of detention. It was bad, but it wasn't toilet scrubbing or children's prison…so, really, it could have been *much* worse.

Principal Demerit dismissed us with a wave of her hand, and Bradley and I scurried out into the hallway, then pressed our backs against the wall, gasping like we'd just been through a terrible ordeal—because we had!

"That was the scariest thing of my life," Bradley said. His eyes were still wide.

"Me, too," I said. "I'll tell you one thing: I am never, ever going to pull anyone's wig off again." I meant it, too. I was also never going to spill a high-sugar energy drink on anyone's shoes. And I was never going to try to mind-control anyone into going away. Because even though the Rats had bad attitudes (as proven by the fact that about five of them had tried to trip me in the hallway that morning alone), what Principal Demerit said was also true: they didn't want to be at Gledhill any more than we wanted them to be there. In fact, right from the start, they'd probably wanted to be there even *less*. This whole time, I'd been trying to fight an injustice that was really nobody's fault—and look where it had gotten me.

"Ummm…hi," said a tiny voice.

Somehow, despite my supersonic hearing (which was possibly the only real power I had besides waking up at 7:14), the very small R.R. Reginald kid called Abby (aka Mouse-Girl) had managed to sneak up behind us on her teeny tiny feet.

"You're Bradley, right? And Clara?"

She was the last person I felt like talking to, so I didn't say anything at first.

"I just wanted to apologize," she said very softly. "For telling on you. I normally hate tattlers. It's just, I was nervous about singing the national anthem. And then, when you changed the music… it was really embarrassing."

She looked down at the floor when she said the last part, and without thinking what I was doing, I reached out and touched her arm.

"Actually, *I'm* sorry," I said. And I really was.

She looked up and smiled shyly. "That's okay,"

she said. "I guess our school started it when Becky pushed the Gator. That wasn't an honorable thing to do *at all.*" She shrugged and looked at her feet again. "Anyway, I have to go help one of the teachers. I'll see you later?"

"Sure," I said, smiling back at her. She disappeared into one of the fourth-grade classes.

"Well…she seems okay," Bradley said, once she was gone. "Maybe the Rats aren't *all* bad after all."

"Maybe they aren't," I agreed, and then my mouth dropped open because there, coming out of the classroom, was Abby, carrying the hugest pile of textbooks I'd ever seen in my life. She smiled at us, shifted the books in her arms as if they were feathers, and headed off down the hall.

Was it possible that Mouse-Girl possessed powers of super strength? Well, it looked like I was probably going to have the rest of the term to find out. And you know what? I didn't even mind that fact so much anymore.

Of course, there was still the matter of Momo, who hadn't forgiven me yet. When I saw her outside, she didn't call me "brat" or throw leaves at me even once. Even though she wasn't moving for another month, I was so lonely and miserable that I felt like she'd already gone.

"Don't worry," my mom kept saying. "Momo loves you. She'll come around. Just be ready to apologize when she does."

And I *was* ready. More than ready, but the days passed. The air got colder. The first snow fell, and still there was no sign of Momo forgiving me.

At least, not until almost two weeks later. It was a Saturday morning. And—big surprise—I woke up at exactly 7:14.

I sighed as I rolled out of bed. Of all the awesome super powers I'd believed I had, *of course* the only one that was real was the most useless of all!

Or was it?

I heard a familiar rattling groan. My dad had been busy with his newest invention—a cordless hair dryer/curling iron combo for my mom so she could multitask while getting ready in the morning—and he *still* hadn't fixed the garage door. Normally, I would have ignored it like usual, but for some reason, my heart started beating faster, and I found myself walking toward the window.

I pulled open the curtains. A fresh blanket of snow had covered everything in the night, but now it was raining on top of the snow. In the still-dark morning, the streetlights reflected off the sleek coat of ice like a mirror. I heard a crunching noise. Coming out of the shadows was a small, hunched figure. Momo! She was balancing along the sidewalk in a purple coat and fluffy white hat.

Where could she be going so early on a Saturday morning, and in such bad weather? I watched her teeter and totter past our house on the slick sidewalk, and as she got closer, I noticed the bag of birdseed under her arm. Of course. She was going to feed the scary birds that lived in the terrible tree near the bus stop. She always worried about them when the weather was bad. I wondered who would do that once she was gone. One thing was for sure, it *wasn't* going to be me.

I kept watching as she shuffled down the icy sidewalk. I was up anyway, and I wanted to keep working on my newest comic strip.

I managed to finish the last panel before the sun came up. By then, twenty minutes had passed. I went back and added more details, then glanced at the clock again. It had been twenty-five minutes. I waited another five for Momo to return, but then I started to worry. It didn't take that long to feed a few scary birds. Something was wrong. I pulled on a pair of socks and went downstairs to get my coat, then I ducked out the still-open garage door and slid down the driveway on the soles of my boots. Up ahead, I could see the sinister, shadowy form of the tree. Under the drizzle of rain and in the gray early-morning light, it looked twice as terrible as usual.

The last thing I wanted to do was walk anywhere near it, and I almost convinced myself that going back to bed would be the smartest thing—after all, Momo had made it pretty clear that she still didn't want to see me—but as I got a few steps closer, I noticed something weird. Momo's coat and hat were on the ground. But where was Momo? It took me a second to realize that she was still inside them…only she was lying down. A few steps more, and I could see that she was moving her arms and legs. The birdseed was spilled all over, and a bunch of ugly birds were walking around her, pecking at it.

"Momo!" I said, breaking into a run, which turned out to be a bad idea. I slipped and fell on my bum, and had to get up and start over. "That's such a weird place to make a snow angel. Why don't you do it on your lawn?" But I think I already knew that she wasn't making snow angels.

She tipped her head back at the sound of my voice. "Clara? What are you doing out here?"

"Looking for you," I said. "I saw you walk past, and when you didn't come back, I got worried."

One of the ugly black birds looked up at me when I got too close to its precious seed. "BA-CAAWWW, BA-CAAAAAWWWW," it squawked loudly, flapping its wings at me.

I flinched, but only a little, then I waved my arms at it threateningly. "Ba-caaw, yourself!" I shouted. "Get lost!"

It retreated to a branch, where it sat hunching its waxy feathers up around its neck and watching me suspiciously. I stomped my foot in the snow and the other birds followed it.

Momo held her hands out to me. "Help me up,

will you, squirt? I'm not making a snow angel. I came out here to feed the birds, like a fool, and I slipped on this patch of ice. I can't seem to get up."

I reached for Momo's hands. "Oof!" she said as I tried to pull her upright. My boots kept slipping against the ice, and every time I'd get her partway up, I'd fall down.

"Go get your dad, will you, kiddo?" she said after a few tries. "I think we need some more muscle."

So I ran as fast as I could, slipping and sliding on the ice all the way back to the house. As soon as I got in the door, I shouted loud—louder than I'd ever shouted before—so loud that my dad said later that he jumped out of bed and made it down the stairs in a single bound before he even realized what was happening.

My dad seemed really scared, which made *me* really scared, but by the time we got back to Momo, she was laughing.

"Good morning, Andrew," she said from the ground, tipping her head back to look at my dad. "I'm in a bit of a bind."

"We'll have you up in no time," he said, putting his hands underneath her armpits and picking her up like she was a doll. "You okay there?" he asked as he set her on her feet, but she didn't even have time to answer before her ankle gave out, sending her falling sideways. My dad caught her and propped her upright again. "I think we'd better get that ankle looked at at the clinic," he said. "Clara, run and ask your mom to bring the car around."

He didn't have to ask me twice. I was already slipping and sliding back toward the house as fast as my boots would carry me—the wind streaming through my hair. Momo needed help, and I wasn't going to let her down.

It was after lunch before my dad and Momo finally made it home from the clinic. I watched through the window as he helped her into her house.

"Well…" my dad said, coming in a few minutes later and taking off his mitts. "The bad news is that Momo's ankle is fractured. But the good news is that the doctors think it should heal quickly, as long as she stays off it. She's also very lucky that you found her when you did, Clara. She could have easily gotten frostbite lying out there in the freezing rain."

"It was very brave of you," my mom agreed. "*Not* that we want you to do it again. Next time you suspect something might be wrong, come get us first."

I promised that I would.

"Momo asked if you'd be free to go over and play cards with her later," my dad said. "To keep her company."

I jumped up out of my chair. Did this mean what I thought it did? Was Momo finally forgiving me?

I should have remembered, though…When you get on Momo's bad side (like the neighbors across the street, who let their cat out without getting it neutered first), you tended to stay there for a *long* time.

"Come in," Momo hollered when I knocked on

211

her back door ten minutes later. "You know better than to wait for an invitation. And I can't get up to let you in." I kicked off my boots and tiptoed into the living room, where Momo was wedged into her reading chair with a cushion. Her fractured ankle was wrapped in a bandage and balanced on a stool.

I could tell she was still mad at me, just by the look on her face—and I knew she had every reason to be. The curtains had been set back on their rod and the shreds of wallpaper on the floor had been cleaned up, but the walls still looked awful. It made me feel so terrible that I barely knew what to say. Thankfully, Momo didn't seem interested in talking.

"We're playing Spit today," she said.

I went to the cupboard and got our two favorite decks of cards—the one with pictures of tropical birds on the back and the one with the sailboats. I shuffled both and handed her the birds. We each put our piles on the coffee table in front of us, with the top cards facing up. Momo barely waited for me to finish before shouting "Spit!" and slapping down her first card in the middle, then her second and third.

"Wait a sec!" I said, but Momo wasn't waiting. She was in a bad mood. And when she's in a bad mood, she's a lean, mean card-playing machine. If I wanted to have any hope of beating her, and maybe even earning her forgiveness, I was going to have to play hard.

We got stuck, yelled "Ready? Spit!" and both flipped over a new starter card. The game went on, with us slapping each other's hands out of the way and shouting at the top of our lungs until Momo slammed down her last card and grinned at me with a gloating, satisfied smile.

I sighed, abandoning my cards on the table.

"Beat you!" she announced, like I didn't already know.

I bit hard on my lip, trying to hold in my disappointment. There's nothing Momo hates more than a sore loser, and I didn't want to give her any more reasons to be mad at me. Plus now that I was warmed up, I *wasn't* planning to lose the next game...or at least I wouldn't have lost it, if there'd been one.

Instead of shuffling her deck, Momo sat back in her chair. "You and I need to talk, don't we?"

I looked down at my lap. "Would you like to go first?" she asked.

I knew it wasn't exactly a question, so I took a deep breath and started the apology I'd been rehearsing for almost two weeks.

"I'm sorry," I said, my voice coming out small. She looked at me like I should go on. "I'm sorry that I let my chinchilla into your house, and that she ate your wallpaper and damaged your curtains. I think she was just trying to climb them to see if there were any raisins at the top, but still…that was wrong. I just wanted you to stay living next door forever."

When I'd finished, Momo was quiet for what felt like a long time. "Okay," she said finally. "Now it's my turn."

She cleared her throat, then blinked a few times, like she was trying to think of the right place to begin.

"I'm sorry, too," she said finally. "I'm sorry that I won't be living next door to you anymore. I'm just as sad about that as you are. You may be nine and I may be eighty…but we're best friends, aren't we?"

I nodded. We were—when she wasn't furious at me.

"Then why don't you just stay?" I asked. I didn't mean for them to, but my eyes had gotten all watery.

Momo stared out the window at the still-icy street. "What do you think would have happened this morning if you hadn't been there to rescue me?" she asked.

I shrugged.

"I might have been in big trouble," she said.

"But I *was* there to rescue you!" I said.

"What if I fall again?" she asked.

"I'll still be here," I answered.

"What about when I start to need help taking the trash out? Or getting up on chairs to change lightbulbs? Or making my supper?"

"I can change lightbulbs," I said. "Trust me, I do it a lot. It's actually easy. And I know how to make Kraft Dinner in the microwave."

Momo smiled. "You were quite the hero this morning," she said. "But I don't need you to be my hero, Clara. I just need you to be my friend."

"I can do both," I pleaded.

"No, kiddo," she said sadly. "You've got too much growing up to do. You can't be looking after an old lady. Even one as young as me." She reached across the card table and took my hand. "So I'm going. And that's that."

A few tears trickled down my cheek. Momo wiped them away and smiled.

"No crying," she said. "Remember? You'll come visit me all the time. And we've still got two weeks. We can't afford to lose focus now. How many ice cream flavors are left?"

"Sixteen," I said sadly.

"Well, then," Momo answered, starting to count on her fingers. "We've got fourteen days. We'll need to double up on Saturday and Sunday, but I think we can do it. Except…" She glanced down at her ankle, suddenly looking discouraged. "I keep forgetting about this stupid thing. I'm not supposed to walk on it. And I'd hate to ask your dad to drive us. We need all his energy focused on fixing that garage door. I like most of his crazy inventions…like the scrambled-egg-o-matic and the self-cleaning litter box he gave me for Christmas. But that garage door is driving me nuts."

I glanced out the window at the snow, feeling discouraged, too. When Momo had said, "That's that," that was *really* that. She was definitely moving and there was nothing I could do but accept it. And as for the ice cream, it seemed pretty hopeless as well. I stared out the window, watching miserably as some kids from down the street ran past with their sleds on their way to the tobogganing hill. Then, as if out of nowhere, an idea came to me—perfectly formed in my mind.

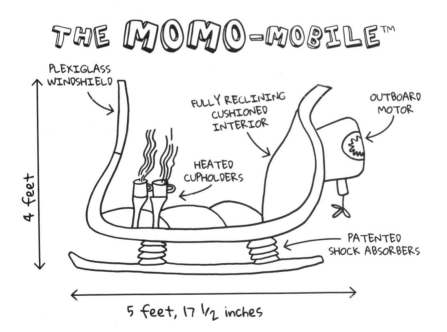

THE MOMO-MOBILE™

PLEXIGLASS WINDSHIELD

FULLY RECLINING CUSHIONED INTERIOR

OUTBOARD MOTOR

HEATED CUPHOLDERS

4 feet

PATENTED SHOCK ABSORBERS

5 feet, 17 ½ inches

Maybe things weren't so hopeless after all.

"Wait here!" I said, jumping up and pulling on my coat. "I'll be back."

True, I didn't have a single super power except for waking up at 7:14...but maybe in the real world, being super wasn't about levitating stuff, having a cool-sounding super-name, and wearing a shiny cape (or even a first-place hundred-meter-dash blue ribbon). After all, there were lots of ways a regular kid could be kind of exceptional.

One way was by acting courageously—especially when you were scared to death (like walking toward the terrible tree in the early morning mist because I had a feeling Momo needed me). Another was by acting honorably, especially when it was hard—like sharing my school with kids I didn't like and who didn't like me back, or letting one of my best friends move far away to a place where she'd play Bingo and maybe be a little bit bored, but at least she'd have people to look after her.

And still a third way was by doing whatever you could to make your friends happy—whether that meant going on a (probably pointless) hunt for pirate treasure in the Save-o-Rama parking lot or finding a way to finish sixteen flavors of ice cream against all the odds…which is just what my dad and I did with the help of an old sleigh we found in the garage, two rolls of duct tape, a chair, and a little imagination.

It may not have been exactly super, but somehow, I had a feeling that even @Cat would have approved.

Acknowledgments

First, I'd like to thank the kid from my 2011 Toronto Public Library workshop who was always drawing superhero cartoons at the back of the room. Your determination to do your own thing was the inspiration for Clara, and if we ever meet again, I owe you a whole bunch of chocolate bars.

Thanks also to YaYa (Diana Bartlett) for having such a special friendship with my family, and for letting me fictionalize her into Momo. For the record, I told the story all backward. We were the ones who moved, and we miss you every day.

Thank you to Rebecca Friedman for her help with the manuscript, and to my top-notch agent, Amy Tompkins, for finding the Clara Humble series its home at Owlkids, where it is being lovingly looked after by a wonderful team, including the awesome and amazing Karen Li, Sarah Howden, Allison MacLachlan, and Karen Boersma.

Thanks to my dad for helping to develop supercat 2.0, to Lisa Cinar for giving @Cat such catitude, to Catherine Dorton for fixing all my spelling mistakes, and to Barb Kelly for her excellent design work.

Huge high-fives to the Canada Council for the Arts and the Toronto Arts Council for their funding support on this project, and for their ongoing support of the arts in Canada.

And of course, hugs to Brent, Grace, and Elliot for being my humans, and ear scratches to Ramona and Stella for being my cats.

COMING SOON

Book 2 in the Clara Humble series!

CLARA HUMBLE

Quiz Whiz

Clara's setting her sights on a new goal: being trivia champion on the *Smarty Pants* game show! Picture it: Clara Humble up on the stage, squaring off against seven other kids to take the *Smarty Pants* crown—and win $1,000 in cold, hard cash…

But it's not an easy challenge, and as the competition heats up, it turns into the age-old schoolyard battle: boys versus girls. People take sides, and it isn't pretty. Will Clara fight dirty to win? And will her friendship with Bradley survive?